P9-BYT-823

Center

A top secret government facility located on a mountain in Colorado. Unparalleled advanced research and testing is conducted by renowned scientists at this state-of-the-art facility.

Collective

A group of secret, yet powerful political leaders who oversee Center activities.

Enforcer

A genetically enhanced human created at Center for the sole purpose of carrying out missions related to national security. Enforcers are highly trained in the arts of assassination, protection and recovery of intelligence related to national security. An Enforcer is to stop at nothing, take whatever extreme measures are required to get the job done.

Dear Harlequin Intrigue Reader,

You won't be able to resist a single one of our May books. We have a lineup so shiver inducing that you may forget summer's almost here!

- *Executive Bodyguard* is the second book in Debra Webb's exciting new trilogy, THE ENFORCERS. For the thrilling conclusion, be sure you pick up *Man of Her Dreams* in June.

- Amanda Stevens concludes her MATCHMAKERS UNDERGROUND series with *Matters of Seduction*. And the Montana McCalls are back, in B.J. Daniels's *Ambushed!*

- We also have two special premiers for you. Kathleen Long debuts in Harlequin Intrigue with *Silent Warning*, a chilling thriller. And LIPSTICK LTD., our special promotion featuring sexy, sassy sleuths, kicks off with Darlene Scalera's *Straight Silver*.

- A few of your favorite Harlequin Intrigue authors have some special books you'll love. Rita Herron's *A Breath Away* is available this month from HQN Books. And, in June, Joanna Wayne's *The Gentlemen's Club* is being published by Signature Spotlight.

Harlequin Intrigue brings you the best in breathtaking romantic suspense with six fabulous books to enjoy. Please write to us—we love to hear from our readers.

Sincerely,

Denise O'Sullivan
Senior Editor
Harlequin Intrigue

DEBRA WEBB

Executive Bodyguard

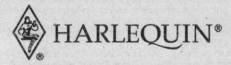

HARLEQUIN®

TORONTO • NEW YORK • LONDON
AMSTERDAM • PARIS • SYDNEY • HAMBURG
STOCKHOLM • ATHENS • TOKYO • MILAN • MADRID
PRAGUE • WARSAW • BUDAPEST • AUCKLAND

If you purchased this book without a cover you should be aware
that this book is stolen property. It was reported as "unsold and
destroyed" to the publisher, and neither the author nor the
publisher has received any payment for this "stripped book."

This book is dedicated to women all over the world—
never forget that anything is possible.

ISBN 0-373-22843-0

EXECUTIVE BODYGUARD

Copyright © 2005 by Debra Webb

All rights reserved. Except for use in any review, the reproduction or
utilization of this work in whole or in part in any form by any electronic,
mechanical or other means, now known or hereafter invented, including
xerography, photocopying and recording, or in any information storage
or retrieval system, is forbidden without the written permission of the
publisher, Harlequin Enterprises Limited, 225 Duncan Mill Road,
Don Mills, Ontario, Canada M3B 3K9.

All characters in this book have no existence outside the imagination of
the author and have no relation whatsoever to anyone bearing the same
name or names. They are not even distantly inspired by any individual
known or unknown to the author, and all incidents are pure invention.

This edition published by arrangement with Harlequin Books S.A.

® and TM are trademarks of the publisher. Trademarks indicated with
® are registered in the United States Patent and Trademark Office, the
Canadian Trade Marks Office and in other countries.

www.eHarlequin.com

Printed in U.S.A.

ABOUT THE AUTHOR

Debra Webb was born in Scottsboro, Alabama, to parents who taught her that anything is possible if you want it badly enough. When her husband joined the military, they moved to Berlin, Germany, and Debra became a secretary in the commanding general's office. By 1985 they were back in the States, and with the support of her husband and two beautiful daughters, Debra took up writing full-time and in 1998 her dream of writing for Harlequin came true. You can write to Debra with your comments at P.O. Box 64, Huntland, Tennessee 37345 or visit her Web site at www.debrawebb.com to find out exciting news about her next book.

Books by Debra Webb

*Colby Agency
**The Specialists
†Colby Agency: Internal Affairs
††The Enforcers

CAST OF CHARACTERS

Cain—An Enforcer, a genetically engineered bodyguard assigned to complete the Lazarus Mission.

Caroline Winters—President of the United States. How can she run the country without putting herself in danger?

Justin Winters—First husband. Is he dead or alive?

Rupert Downy—The senior adviser to the president. Is he friend or foe?

Dr. Dennis Patrick—One of Caroline's oldest friends. Can he help her put her marriage back together?

Steven Redmond—Vice president of the United States. Why is he trying to usurp Caroline's authority?

Howard Copeland and Greg Levitt—Two of Caroline's most trusted Secret Service agents.

Director Richard O'Riley—Center director. He has the power to put men and women into the Oval Office.

Congressman Terrence Winslow—The head of the Collective. He leaves the day-to-day operations to O'Riley. No one can connect him to trouble at Center.

Dr. Waylon Galen—The original creative mind behind the Enforcers.

Mr. Dupree—Is he maintaining the integrity of the intelligence he passes on to Director O'Riley?

Prologue

Three months earlier

Justin Winters clutched the briefcase in his lap with white-knuckled intensity as the plane dipped and then jerked upward yet again. He swallowed back the paralyzing fear climbing into his throat.

The Cessna's pilot struggled to keep the plane aloft but Justin had a feeling the fight was lost already.

The plane was going down.

He stared at the briefcase. The contents would never reach Caroline.

She would never know the truth.

He wouldn't be able to save her.

His heart rammed against his rib cage and a sinking sensation dragged at the pit of his stomach as the plane plummeted. Voices screamed around him as the other three aboard shouted hysterically and braced for the crash.

Justin did neither.

There was no point.
He was going to die.
They all were…

Chapter One

Present day
Ghost Mountain, Colorado

"You're certain the danger is real." Congressman Terrence Winslow phrased the question as if it were a statement, yet O'Riley knew he was asking...needing reassurances.

"I'm as certain as I can be," Richard O'Riley replied with a negligent shrug. "I can only go on the intelligence we've gathered thus far. But, if you're asking me to stake my reputation on it, then consider it done. I have complete confidence in our sources."

That was the bottom line for O'Riley. Winslow, however, wanted someone to nail to the wall if this operation turned out badly. As director of Center operations, the hide that would get nailed was O'Riley's. It was the nature of the beast. He could take the heat, otherwise he would have gotten out of this business a long time ago.

National security secrets, lying, leading a double life—it was all a part of the deal. It was who he was. Who he'd always been. A man didn't reach the top of the food chain in a lethally complex environment like this without having accepted a number of facts along the way. Truth was vastly overrated and the only difference between a bad guy and a good guy was getting caught.

Center, an advanced research and development facility carefully tucked away in the Colorado mountains, represented one of the nation's most valuable assets as well as one of its biggest secrets. Only a handful of people were aware of Center's existence and its mission. Those chosen few were either employed by Center or members belonging to the Collective, a council charged with the oversight of Center's long-term goals.

The research Center conducted remained unparalleled by any individual or country on the planet. The creation of the Enforcers represented their greatest achievement to date. Yet, few could ever know.

"Then we have no other choice." Winslow clasped the arms of his chair and prepared to push to his feet. "I'll set things in motion on my end." He stood and waited for O'Riley to respond, since he was now officially off the proverbial hook.

As chairman of the Collective, Winslow possessed the authority to make the final decision. The entire committee had already voted, giving their joint blessing to whatever action Center deemed necessary. Winslow, on the other hand, had hesitated, wanting to consider the matter carefully—wanting to cover his genteel hindquarter.

Removing a president from office was not an everyday affair. Certainly not an initiative to be taken lightly.

"Congressman," O'Riley began, rising to match his

stance, "it is the right thing to do. The only thing to do. There is no other way to protect her. We can't lose her now. You know we can't trust Redmond to take care of our needs, much less the country's. He is less than reliable and has far too many connections to the wrong lobbyist groups."

Winslow quirked an eyebrow. "And yet this very action would put our esteemed vice president in the perfect position to destroy us."

"Only temporarily," O'Riley countered. "The interim will give us time to determine the source of the threat. Whoever is behind this plot is getting closer. Too close. Close enough to strike at any moment. We have to act now. Everything is set. There's no reason for delay. The sooner we take action, the sooner we will have our president back into power and all will be as it should be. Acting on a temporary basis the VP won't make any unexpected or intolerable moves. This is the only way."

The threat to the president was all too real and, sadly, appeared to be coming from within her own trusted circle. That scenario required a certain response. No matter how beefed up her security detail, a threat from within her own ranks was difficult to see coming. The strike could come from any member of that very security detail or her closest confidant. She had to be protected, ultimately safeguarding Center's best interests.

Winslow passed a hand over his face. "I hope to God you're right. I'll be at the hotel in Boulder awaiting word. I don't plan to return to Washington until…this is done." He moved toward the door but stopped as he reached it. His solemn gaze settled heavily onto O'Riley. "You know this could end badly. Could ruin everything," he said grimly, second thoughts obviously plaguing him still.

O'Riley braced his hands on his desk and stared directly into that somber gaze. "Yes, Terry, I know the risks involved." Better than anyone, he didn't add. "But this is a Level VII operation. Our choices are sorely limited."

Without saying more, the congressman closed the door behind him. What was the point in further discussion? This had to be done…O'Riley knew it and so did the Collective, including Winslow.

He blew out a breath and straightened. His door opened again but, he saw thankfully, it wasn't Winslow, it was Dupree. O'Riley had asked Center's senior intelligence analyst to stand by when Winslow had arrived ahead of schedule this afternoon.

"Is he ready?" O'Riley asked, not giving Dupree a chance to launch his own rhetoric. He didn't want to hear any ifs, buts or maybes. O'Riley wanted a simple yes or no.

"Forty-eight hours," Dupree said thinly, fully aware that this was not the answer his superior wanted to hear. "Medical insists they need two more days to ensure full readiness."

Swearing hotly not once but twice, O'Riley dropped back into his chair. "What the hell do they need forty-eight additional hours for? They've had two weeks. We're running out of time here."

Dupree blinked but didn't falter a step as he generally did. "Well, sir, they...they think the additional time is necessary for—"

O'Riley held up a hand, stalling the explanation Dupree had no doubt demanded from the chief medical officer upon hearing the request. But O'Riley didn't give a damn about the excuses. He wasn't stupid enough to ignore Medical's request. If the time was necessary to the success of the operation, then so be it. He didn't have to like it.

"Forty-eight hours," O'Riley said pointedly. "Not a single minute more. I want him ready to go by this time on Wednesday." He shook his head. "No excuses, no delays." He glanced at the digital clock on his desk. 3:30 p.m. "Is that crystal-clear?"

Dupree nodded jerkily, then caught himself. "Of course. I'll pass your orders along, sir. Three-thirty on Wednesday."

O'Riley considered the steps necessary to ensure the president's survival for the next forty-eight hours. Without an Enforcer in place he couldn't guarantee anything. But his contact, a senior White House official, would do all he could. O'Riley was certain of that.

Would it be enough?

"Just one more thing," he said to Dupree before the harried analyst could make his escape.

Dupree turned back to him, one hand already poised on the doorknob. "Yes, sir?"

"Tell Medical that I'll require a full demonstration. Visual, oral and intellectual."

"Of course."

Dupree didn't waste another second getting out of

O'Riley's office. He would pass along the information to Medical and preparations would be made. Forty-eight hours from now, a plan the top analysts and strategists belonging to Center had devised would see fruition.

If their plan failed…all would be lost. But it was the only chance they had. If an Enforcer couldn't protect the president, then her death was clearly divine providence. He shrugged off the thought. That would not be the case. God was always on the side of right…of the good guys.

They were the good guys.

The ends justified the means.

East Virginia Mountains
Mattson Family Retreat

CAROLINE WINTERS stood at the front window gazing out over the secluded property that had belonged to her father, and to his father before him. She'd come to this mountain cabin dozens of times as a child growing up. Between sessions of Congress she and her family had escaped to this remote location to relax and enjoy simply being. As a respected member of Congress, her father had devoted his life to his country. Their regular family outings were among her most treasured memories of her father.

But even this far up the mountain and this deep in the woods she could not escape the cold, harsh reality awaiting her in the real world.

"Madam President, we're going to need that decision soon—this evening."

Before turning to the man who'd spoken, Caroline

watched two men belonging to her security detail make their quarter-hour rounds outside. There were more than a dozen Secret Service agents out there, and four more inside, one stationed at each entry to the two-story cabin, and the agent in charge posted on point, not more than ten feet or so from her side.

She couldn't escape the truth.

Caroline squared her shoulders and blinked twice, ruing the damned tears determined to swell each time she thought of the truth she could no longer deny.

Justin was dead.

She understood that was the most probable case.

Part of the plane's wreckage had been found within days of the accident. But not all. Not one of the bodies had been recovered. She shuddered as exhaustion conspired with dread, dragging her emotions back into a whirlwind of desperate confusion.

Her husband was dead.

She must have imagined the calls…the letter.

But the voice…the handwriting…it had been his. She knew her own husband's voice. For God's sake, they had known each other their entire adult lives, had been close friends a great deal of that time. She'd devoured letter after letter from him while he had served as an aide to the attaché in the Middle East. Making a mistake about his handwriting wasn't likely.

And still those who had supported her all through her campaign, who had been there for her when her husband's plane had gone down only three months after her inauguration, now doubted her mental stability.

She was the first female president of the United States. She'd served a full term and part of a second one as a U.S. senator prior to that. No one had expected her to win, but she had. She'd won by a wide enough margin to startle her male counterparts, usurping her predecessor as if he'd managed nothing at all during his four years in office.

The people were counting on her. How could she let them down? The answer was simple…she could not.

"Caroline." From behind her Rupert Downy, her senior advisor, rested a hand upon her right shoulder and brought the tension in the room down a notch by using her first name. "I know this is very difficult—"

She turned to face him, the move forcing his hand to fall back to his side. "No, Rupert," she returned succinctly, "living the rest of my life knowing that the final words I said to him were harsh and hurtful is difficult." She lifted her chin in defiance of the emotions twisting her insides and stared him straight in the eye. She refused to allow the memories of that last morning the opportunity to surface yet again. "Admitting that I may no longer be fit to hold office is simply a lie."

Rupert bowed his head for a moment, most likely to get a firmer grasp on his patience or perhaps his own emotions. Caroline closed her eyes and shook her head slowly from side to side. She was behaving petulantly. Not a good thing in a commander in chief.

"I apologize, Rupert," she offered wearily when he remained silent. He had her best interests at heart. That was his job…and she trusted him. Rupert had been a part of her family for as long as she could remember. Though her mother had never remarried after her father's death, Caroline was very much aware that there was something between Rupert and her mother. Neither of them had ever acted upon it. That truth suddenly felt like such a shame. Life was so very fleeting.

"I'm acting on emotion," she went on, knowing he deserved better than to be her whipping post. He met her gaze and she dragged in a heavy breath. There was no way around what was to come. She could either face it head-on or let it sneak up on her from the rear. Caroline had never been one to hide from a battle—especially not when truth was on her side. "Let's discuss the matter and try and reach some sort of decision."

Rupert turned to the agent posted in the room. "Excuse us for a few minutes, Agent Copeland."

Agent Copeland nodded once and left the expansive family room that occupied the full width of the right side of the ground floor. He wouldn't go far. Perhaps into the foyer or across the hall to the kitchen or dining room allowing privacy without his being more than a few feet away. His orders would not allow him to be out of visual and audible range at the same time or to be more than thirty feet from her at any given moment. Since the Code Red had gone into effect, he or one of his relief agents had even taken to sleeping in the study that connected to her bedroom.

Taking a long weekend retreat here, away from the mounting tension at the White House, had been a necessity. Caroline sat down on the plaid sofa that had been a part of this country home for as long as she could remember, only the upholstery had changed from time to time. Justin had overseen the remodeling of the cabin and its well-worn furnishing only a couple of years ago. She closed her eyes and banished the bittersweet memory. That had been the way of it with her and Justin. Bittersweet. Just another thing that only she would understand…that she could share with no one. Well, except Dennis, who happened to be a friend she'd known almost as long as Justin. But there was no time to dwell on that now.

Settling her gaze on her trusted confidant, Caroline urged, "Tell me what you think I should do, Rupert." She waited for what she knew would be his answer. There was no putting off the issue any longer.

He sat down directly across from her in an overstuffed side chair, upholstered in a nice navy to coordinate with the red, gold and deep-blue plaid of the sofa. "They're not going to let this go." He braced his forearms on his spread knees and clasped his hands together. She noticed for the first time how very old her dear friend looked just now. Had the past three months done that to him? It had certainly taken its toll on her.

"Redmond is adamant," Rupert went on. "He has the whole Cabinet stirred up. Anything we do or say at this point will make us look bad. He has you on tape."

Caroline winced. She'd had a private meeting with her vice president two weeks ago. She'd shared with him the phone calls and the letter—the letter that oddly had gone missing before she could show it to anyone else. A rundown of incoming and outgoing calls on all lines at the White House as well as her cell phone had shown no unidentified calls, lending credence to the idea that her claims were unfounded.

But she had not imagined the incidents. She had heard Justin's voice…had read his handwritten note. But she couldn't prove any of it.

Even more damning were the official appointments she'd forgotten lately. A frown furrowed her brow. She never forgot meetings. Never had to be ushered to an appointment at the last minute. It was hard to believe she had in recent weeks. But the calendar proved her oversights. Even the calendar in her personal digital assistant (PDA) had refuted her insistence that she had not known about the appointments.

She told herself that someone had made a mistake and slipped a new calendar into her PDA and on her desk. Even her personal assistant and staffers reluctantly admitted that they had known about the appointments. Everyone had known about them but her. It felt precisely like a conspiracy…an attempt to make her look incompetent. But that line of thinking was childish and self-serving. Her staff was highly professional. She'd handpicked most of those surrounding her. Why would anyone do something as foolish as setting her up to look incompetent? What would it accomplish?

Other than to make her appear unfit for the office she held.

"If you invoke the Twenty-Fifth Amendment yourself, then you will be in charge to some degree."

Her head moved from side to side before his statement fully penetrated the haze of confusion clouding her
brain. "That would mean—"

"That would mean," he cut in gently, "that you recognize you need a break to pull yourself together. It would
be *temporary,*" he added with an emphatic nod of his
head. "*You* would hold the power to set a time limit on
that leave of absence. I would recommend two weeks
for a start. This would take the heat off while throwing
a bone to the hounds nipping at your heels."

She didn't like this. She didn't like it at all. "And
what are the people who put me in this office supposed
to think?" She rocketed to her feet, rubbed her damp
palms against her slacks and started to pace. "They en-
trusted me with the highest office in the land, I can't let
them down. Not without just cause. I have not failed to
fulfill the requirements of my post."

Rupert propped his chin on his hands and considered
her words for a time. "I agree. But the issue is not your
demeanor at the moment or whether you've fulfilled the
obligations of your post. It's about your actions over the
past weeks and months. The little things plucked from
here and there. We have to face facts here. If we don't
do it, *they* will, and then the power will belong to the
other side."

Caroline threw her hands up. "When did Steve Redmond become the other side? The man I chose—asked
personally—to be my running mate?" Even as she made
the demands she knew Rupert was right. Within days of
his taking office, her vice president's personality had

changed. He was no longer the kind, enthusiastic supporter she had thought him to be. He argued her every point, blatantly attempted to cast her in a bad light before both the House and the Senate. Considering what he had the courage to say in her presence she scarcely dared think what he said behind her back. Now, if the rumors were true, he'd set his aim on the public by leaking suggestions to the press that she was falling apart.

The man epitomized the term *traitor.*

He had betrayed her.

Just as Justin had.

Caroline pushed that last thought from her mind. She refused to replay those memories. The past was gone…dead. She shuddered but quickly caught herself and steeled her emotions.

Rupert stood, tucked his hands into his trouser pockets and jingled his change. Despite present circumstances she almost smiled, remembering the dozens and dozens of other times he'd done that very thing. "I have a bad feeling that he was always on the other side. We were either too blind to see it or simply didn't want to. He was an excellent choice as a running mate. Drew in the older male votes when your being female would never have garnered votes from those old codgers."

Maybe Rupert was right. Maybe she hadn't wanted to see Redmond for what he was. Well, it was definitely too late now. She perched back onto the edge of the couch. Most likely her trusted friend was right about the other as well. Maybe she did need a break from everything. If a simple vacation had been sufficient she wouldn't be in this predicament now. Nothing had changed the feelings of dread and anxiety she suffered, not even medication. Dennis, Dr. Patrick, one of her oldest and dearest friends, had prescribed a mild sedative for temporary use. It hadn't helped. Not really. Nor did it change the way she felt. No one would ever convince her that she hadn't heard her dead husband's voice on the phone or read his handwriting in the form of a faxed note.

And yet, looking back, was she really sure of what she'd heard and seen? Could her mind be playing tricks on her? The search team had deemed the crash unsurvivable. Her husband, along with four others counting the pilot, were dead.

Had the long years of overachieving and hard work going all the way back to high school finally caught up with her? Or was it merely guilt? Did a part of her desperately want the opportunity to change the last words she'd spoken to her husband?

She moved to where Rupert stood and held out her hands. He placed his in them without hesitation. The warmth and concern she saw in his eyes firmed her resolve.

"I know you're right. Better to be in charge of the situation than the other way around. As it happens, I'm still in charge and I intend to work this situation to my advantage. What's our first step?"

Rupert smiled and nodded once. "You dictate a letter indicating that you…" His voice trailed off for a moment and he cleared his throat. "A letter indicating that you feel the need to relinquish power for a period of two weeks, and say that at the end of that time you will determine if an additional commitment is needed."

She swallowed back the bile rising in her throat and moistened her lips. She'd worked so hard to get to this point, had so many plans for the nation. How could this happen? How could she allow it to happen?

Rupert obviously read the hesitancy in her eyes. "Women came out to vote for you in masses, Caroline. It was those votes that pushed you over the top. I'll wager there isn't a female in the country who won't understand what you've been through and sympathize completely."

He was right again. She knew he was. But that didn't make the decision any easier.

She drew in a deep, bolstering breath and nodded her agreement. "Call in my immediate staff. Let's get this done."

As Rupert went to do as she'd asked, Caroline uttered a silent, urgent prayer. *Dear God, let this be the right thing for our great nation.*

O'RILEY WATCHED intently as Dr. Fitzgerald unraveled the final layer of gauze bandage from the Enforcer's face. Congressman Winslow stood at O'Riley's side, his gaze, too, riveted on the unveiling.

The Enforcer's name was Cain. He was their first genetically engineered creation. A near-perfect human. His body's incredible ability to heal itself from almost anything practically overnight had enabled the necessary—extensive—cosmetic surgery.

"You're sure using Cain is not a mistake?" Winslow asked under his breath.

O'Riley wished there was a simple answer to that question. Cain was a truly incredible man. Strong, highly intelligent, a photographic memory and trained like no other agent or operative on the planet. Enforcers possessed cutting-edge skills in every manner of defense, were fluent in more than a dozen languages and had elevated sensory perceptions that bordered on psychic ability. But none of those reasons had set Cain apart from the others. All Enforcers possessed those skills.

Cain had two things that the others didn't. The exact physical build and coloring required for the mission. And, the uncanny, almost eerie ability to mimic anything he heard. He was the only Enforcer with that particular skill. The others could learn to imitate speech, but not like Cain. His imitation was no imitation. It was real. Hell, the man could even fool a voice analyzer.

"He's the only one for the job," O'Riley replied to his nervous leader. "No one else has the right build or the mimicking ability to be ready on this kind of short notice." Not to mention his unequalled photographic memory.

Even with that knowledge, O'Riley understood Winslow's hesitation. It wasn't as if he hadn't considered the one problem related to utilizing Cain. He had— at length. Cain, being their first, also bore the one mistake made by the creative minds behind the Enforcers.

He lacked any measurable level of human emotion.

O'Riley had to admit that Cain had learned to compensate for the disadvantage, still, he more often proceeded on the basis of single-minded determination and primal instinct than on reason and assessment.

They had no time to properly prepare anyone else, even if one of the others had met the physical requirements.

The only complex step that had been necessary to ensure Cain's readiness was the plastic surgery to get the facial features right. Just the right scarring had taken care of other telltale indicators that he might be an impostor. Giving him a new set of fingerprints had been a fairly simple laser procedure that still boggled O'Riley's mind. Enough scarring was purposely left to facilitate their game plan. Medical had even come up with an injection that would fool any DNA tests that might unknowingly be performed. The injection would only last for seven days before another would be required. Still, like everything else at Center, it was ingenious.

"Just remember," Winslow said as the final strip of gauze was unwound, "his selection was your decision."

O'Riley grunted. Wasn't it always? Just like the other time they had used Cain in a situation where a partner would not be available to temper his actions, this was necessary. His mission was simple. Get close to the principal and keep her safe at all costs while maintaining his cover.

The doctor stepped away, fully revealing Cain sitting on the end of the treatment table.

Winslow's breath caught sharply. "Merciful God in heaven," he murmured.

O'Riley smiled.

Perfect.

"Amazing job, Fitzgerald," he said to the beaming doctor. "No way will anyone ever suspect that this is not Justin Winters."

Chapter Two

Caroline stared long and hard at the letter her secretary had transcribed. Tension thickened around her as her gaze slid lower to linger on the signature line. If she signed this document there was no turning back. Section Four of the Twenty-Fifth Amendment would be invoked, relieving her of authority and placing the safekeeping of this nation in the hands of the vice president.

It was only temporary, she reminded herself. Two weeks. Fourteen days. Then, unless she confessed to some continued lack in her ability or someone could prove her incompetence and manipulate a majority vote of the Cabinet, she would resume the office.

But was it the right thing to do?

The citizens counted on her to do the right thing. To make decisions as to their best interests. She thought about her father and knew without doubt that he would never have relinquished power in this manner. Certain death would have been all that could have kept him from executing his duties. She'd always considered herself cut from that same cloth. How could she feel so uncertain now? So, out of place in her own skin?

The voice…the letter came back to her in a mad rush, filling her ears with the sound of Justin's voice, blurring her eyes with the sting of emotion as she envisioned the bold strokes of his handwriting. How could she have imagined such things? Surely she was stronger than that. It wasn't as if she and Justin had—

"Caroline."

Rupert's voice tugged her from the painful thoughts. She looked up as he crossed the room. He'd insisted that everyone give her some privacy while she gathered her thoughts and executed this final executive order.

"Yes." He only called her by her first name when no one was around to hear the familiarity between them or when he needed her full attention and it did not appear forthcoming. Rupert stood staunchly on formality and he darn sure didn't want anyone thinking he'd only gotten the job because he'd been a close friend of her father's. She smiled as her gaze met his, but the expression quickly slipped. Something was wrong. Her pulse reacted instantly to the combination of worry and excitement in his eyes. She rose from her chair, leaving the letter on the desk…forgotten. "What's happened?"

"Caroline." He took her by the shoulders. "They've found him."

For a second that turned into five she couldn't fathom what he meant by the simple statement. They'd found whom? Then she knew.

"Where?" The single word whooshed out on the last of the oxygen in her lungs.

"I don't know all the details yet." Emotion glistened in his eyes. "I just know that Justin is alive. He's in a hospital in Mexico City. We've got Air Force One standing by to take you there now. The vice president has been apprised of the situation. We should leave now."

Justin was alive.

Her heart leapt. Thank God.

Caroline strode from the room, Rupert at her side. Her security detail fell into step with her. She didn't question the second chance she'd abruptly been given. Didn't slow to analyze or even ask about the few details that Rupert might or might not know. Justin was alive. That's all that mattered.

She climbed into the waiting armored SUV and the rest of the entourage moved into place without hesitation. Similar vehicles assembled in front of as well as to the rear of the one in which she and Rupert rode. All but two members of her security detail would be in tow. All other staffers, other than her personal secretary, remained behind.

The familiar comfort of the cabin that had been in her family for more than half a century faded out of sight as they moved down the long gravel drive.

The letter typewritten on the distinguished presidential letterhead that revealed her professed vulnerability lay unsigned and forgotten on her desk. She should have destroyed it before she rushed away. But she wouldn't think of that until much later.

By then it would be too late.

Unspecified Location

"How could you have allowed this to happen?" He glared at the other man allowing him to see as well as hear how deeply displeased he was. Fury whipped through him, making him want to tear the man's head off with his bare hands. This sort of mistake was intolerable.

"There *were* no survivors," the pathetic excuse of a man argued plaintively. "We searched the crash area. The pilot was dead. The aircraft—"

"But you didn't track down the other bodies."

He shook his head in defeat. "We thought they'd burned up or were scattered over the countryside. The condition of the aircraft—"

"Yet you didn't bother to verify that possibility."

The man shook his head once more. "There just wasn't any way they could have survived," he offered thinly.

"And yet Justin Winters did." And he knew. Winters had double-crossed them. He had evidence of what they were up to. That evidence could not reach the enemy's hands. Though most likely any tangible evidence had been destroyed in the crash, Winters could very well tell what he'd seen and heard. That would be a somewhat softer blow, but the impact would still be far too great for comfort.

A final decision had to be made now.

If she learned the truth, then it would only be a matter of hours or minutes before the Collective was informed.

He couldn't let that happen.

"Justin Winters is not to leave that country alive." He fixed his underling with a gaze that left no room for question. "I want anyone who has had contact with him to this point dead. Today. Do you understand?"

"I understand."

Before he could hurry away to carry out his new orders one last point needed to be made.

"Your continued failures," he said, garnering the man's full attention once more, "won't be tolerated."

CAROLINE WAITED in the hospital administrator's office while the doctor working on Justin's case was cleared for access. Rupert sat next to her while Agent Copeland remained near the door. The administrator, Mr. Ramirez, had urged Caroline to permit a briefing on her husband's condition before seeing him. She had agreed, though she wasn't pleased about the delay. A part of her wanted to rant at the administrator and his staff, to tell them that she couldn't care less at the moment what anyone had to say. She needed to see Justin. To verify with her own eyes that he was alive.

But she said nothing of the kind. Her every action, every word, reflected on the country she represented. She would not fall down on her duty now. Calm: she had to remain calm and composed. Rupert had already brought her up to speed with what he knew, which wasn't much. The details he had received had been sketchy at best.

"President Winters," Ramirez said, drawing her from the disturbing thoughts, "I am so sorry to keep you waiting." He rushed into the room with a man in tow who wore a white lab coat and black wire rim glasses that sat askew on his face. "Dr. Hernandez will give you an update now."

Mr. Ramirez settled into the chair behind his wide desk, leaving a flustered Dr. Hernandez standing in the middle of the large office looking entirely at a loss.

"Thank you, Dr. Hernandez," Caroline offered in hopes of setting him at ease. "I appreciate your time." She moved to the edge of her seat, unable to subdue the tension ripping through her. "Please tell me how Justin is doing."

The doctor cleared his throat. "Mr. Winters is doing…very well," he said, his English only slightly halting.

"It's been three months." She needed some explanation as to how he had been lost for this much time. "Has he been here this whole time? Is he fully recovered from whatever injuries he sustained in the accident?"

The administrator jumped in to provide the answer to her first question. "Oh, no, Madam President. We now know that for nearly three weeks he wandered in the mountains not so far from the crash site. One of our citizens found him while moving his herd of goats to a new grazing location."

Caroline nodded, her emotions reeling beneath the serene exterior she worked hard to present. "What sort of condition was he in at the time?"

"Very bad," the doctor said gravely. "We were certain he would not live. He had no identification and could not speak. The authorities came and took fingerprints but there is much scarring and the prints were not

usable. But his overall size and description fit one of…"
He cleared his throat. "His description matched that of
a criminal the authorities had been searching for for
many years now. We assumed—wrongly of course—
that he was this very bad man."

"And yet you attempted to save his life." She needed
to understand how this delay in their identifying him
happened. It seemed unreasonable. However, the last
thing she wanted was to appear ungrateful.

"There were answers the police needed. His survival
was very important. Apparently the man they sought
knew the location of others they hoped to apprehend."

"So his condition improved with your care?" Caroline's heart pounded so hard she could scarcely catch her
breath. "He's better?"

The doctor nodded enthusiastically. "But he awoke
from the coma only yesterday." His expression faltered
a little. "Of course we were very upset to learn that we
had considered your fine husband a criminal. We swiftly
amended the situation."

"Coma?" She and Rupert exchanged glances. This
sounded worse all the time. And she felt quite certain
that those in charge had been seriously unsettled when
they realized who they had held here, practically under
house arrest, for all this time.

"He fell into a coma the same day he arrived," the administrator explained. "We were not certain if he would
return to us. As soon as he told us his real name and his
story was verified we contacted your government."

Caroline wanted to get past that for now. She needed

to know more about her husband's current condition. She knew that the prognosis for a comatose patient was most often uncertain. Some woke up, others didn't.

"His many injuries healed well while he was in the coma," Dr. Hernandez went on. "Sometimes the mind goes into a coma so that the body can focus fully on healing itself. This is the case with your husband, I believe."

Dozens of horrifying images flitted past her mind's eye. "How badly wounded was he?" She didn't recall an answer to that question…was the evasion a stall tactic of some sort?

"A number of fractured bones, serious head trauma, and some burns to his hands," the doctor related.

That's why the fingerprints weren't usable, she guessed. "Does he understand who he is? Fully, I mean." It seemed logical that he did on some level since the hospital had known to contact the U.S. ambassador here in Mexico.

"Yes," Hernandez responded quickly. "He woke up asking for you."

Relief flooded Caroline. She held back the sob that surged into her throat. "May I see him now?" She didn't want to wait any longer. She knew all she needed to.

The doctor turned to the administrator who still looked uncertain.

"Is there something else?" Rupert pressed. "Something more we should know first?"

Her trusted friend and advisor had voiced the very concerns tearing at her. Something wasn't quite right.

"Mr. Winters," the administrator began, "has lost a

good deal of his memory. It is doubtful that he will regain it."

"You may find him forgetful and having to learn some things he once knew over again," the doctor added. "He...he is not the same man you last saw."

En route to Mexico Caroline had mentally and physically prepared herself for this moment. She had shored up any doubts by telling that tiny fragile voice whispering in her ear that she could face anything. That no matter her husband's circumstances she would charge in, bring him home and all would be as it should be once more.

But now all that went out the window.

She stood, everyone in the room moved to attention. "I want to see him now."

"I think that would be the best thing," Rupert offered congenially, already moving toward the door.

Caroline couldn't work up any regret at the edge in her tone as she'd issued the demand. Her stomach had tied itself in knots. Her nerves had frayed—enough was enough. She could draw her own conclusions as to Justin's condition.

Mr. Ramirez and Dr. Hernandez led the way. Caroline, Rupert and her security detail followed close behind. The chosen route from the administrator's office to Justin's room had been cleared and approved for her passage. In truth the entire hospital as well as a large area around it had been prepared for her arrival.

The journey down the long corridor to the bank of elevators was wrought with tension. Inside the car that would take them upward it wasn't any better. A stiff jerk and then a smooth rise to their destination. With every passing second Caroline's heart beat faster, her respiration grew more shallow. She had to keep telling herself again and again that this was real, not a dream.

On the third floor the hospital administrator paused outside a closed door. "We've had one of our security officers sitting with him since we learned his identity," he explained as if he feared the guard's presence would be questioned. "A number of your agents are with him now as well."

"Thank you, Mr. Ramirez," Rupert returned. "We sincerely appreciate the additional effort on your part. Your staff has been more than kind. We appreciate all you've done."

Ever the statesman. Caroline was never more thankful for Rupert's presence than she was now. She felt reasonably certain that she could not have done this alone. If they'd had a guard with Justin since they'd learned his true identity, what precautions had they taken when he was thought to be a criminal? The picture of him shackled to the bed made her stomach clench.

Ramirez nodded and pushed open the door. He remained outside while the doctor accompanied Caroline and Rupert into the room. Four Secret Service agents flanked all sides of the room. A fifth man, obviously Hispanic, stood stoically near the bed.

The head of the bed was raised enough that the patient sat upright. A crisp white sheet draped his lower body, banding across his waist. The part of his upper torso visible above the sheet was clad in a printed cotton hospital gown.

Caroline's heart lurched when her gaze settled on the blue one that was as familiar to her as her own hazel eyes. She rushed to his bedside and threw her arms around her husband. "Justin, thank God." She couldn't manage anything else. He was alive and that was all that mattered at the moment. She had so many things she wanted to say to him, so many apologies for the hurtful words. But all of that could wait.

"I was certain I would never see you again," he whispered, his usually smooth voice too deep and gravelly.

Caroline drew back and studied him. She bit her lips together to keep from commenting on the difference. She forced a smile. "I'm here now. I'm sorry I wasn't able to find you sooner." She shook her head slowly from side to side. "The search went on for weeks. They were certain there were no survivors. They only found…" She didn't have to say the rest, he would know.

He nodded. "I understand. I don't know how I survived. I can't remember anything about the crash or the weeks after. It's as if I suddenly woke up yesterday with no memory of anything since I left…you."

Caroline almost winced at the last. Did he remember the hurtful words she'd flung at him? Was that why he seemed so distant now? Tears crowded into her throat. Life was so fragile. She had learned that lesson the hard way when she had lost her father. She had known better than to risk allowing that kind of no-going-back scene to go down. The idea that they might never know what had caused the crash gained full realization. The investigation had reached no conclusive explanation. They had all hoped that if a survivor were found he would be able to explain what had happened, or at least shed some light on the final moments. The so-called black box had rendered nothing.

Clearly they would never know what had happened or whether the incident was an act of sabotage.

The number of others present in the room suddenly annoyed her. She needed time alone with her husband. Time to set things straight. To unburden her heart. To seek forgiveness.

She took his hand in hers and squeezed it gently. Her expression fell as the rough feel of his fingers and dry texture of his skin invaded her senses.

He noticed, his posture instantly stiffening.

Caroline dredged up another smile and refrained from looking down at the hand she held. "Let's go home, Justin."

He nodded. "I've been waiting for you all this time."

All other thought vanished, nothing else mattered. She had let Justin down. But God had granted her a second chance. She would make things right again…somehow.

She turned to Dr. Hernandez. "I can't thank you enough, Doctor. I hope you will let me know if there is ever anything I can do for you or this hospital." She offered the doctor an appreciative smile. "I am greatly in your debt."

Rupert made the necessary arrangements to depart Mexico City. En route aboard Air Force One with Justin resting comfortably in a reclining position, her senior advisor brought up the subject she'd allowed to drift to the farthest recesses of her brain during the past few hours.

"Now, more than ever, I believe that a short vacation is necessary." He leaned forward and spoke for her ears only. "You and Justin need time...alone."

Caroline agreed. He would get no argument from her. However, this changed everything in her opinion. "I'll take some time, but I won't be initiating the Twenty-Fifth." There were other things she needed to attend to as well. Like the speech for the graduating class of her high school alma mater.

"Understandable," Rupert allowed. "I see no reason to go that far under the circumstances. They'll chalk your forgetfulness and insistence that Justin was alive up to women's intuition and leave it at that. Redmond certainly won't pursue the issue."

Caroline's jaw hardened. Redmond. How had she ever been so completely fooled by the man? He would not win this battle. Perhaps he considered her a fragile female incapable of fighting back, but he was wrong. She was far stronger than he suspected. She would fight back. And she would win.

"One way or another I'm going to take Redmond down a couple of notches. I want a meeting with him the moment we return to D.C."

Rupert lifted a skeptical brow. "Let's not be hasty, Madam President."

"I think the problem is that I haven't been hasty enough.

I should have nipped this problem in the bud weeks ago. I don't need my own people working against me."

Rupert flared his hands in question. "I agree. But he is rather vindictive when pushed into a corner. He'll come out fighting."

"I wouldn't want it any other way," Caroline concluded. She was more than ready for this battle. With Justin safe she intended to focus fully on squaring away the little ripples of unrest Redmond had set off in her Cabinet. "He won't win this battle," she said with complete confidence.

A smile pulled across Rupert's face. "I never thought he would."

Other than her extended security detail, the only member of Caroline's staff who had accompanied her on Air Force One on this trip was her personal secretary. She said to Rupert, "I think I'll take care of some necessary dictation while Justin is sleeping. Get in touch with Aaron and have him set up that press conference. I want the world to know this good news right away. We won't involve Justin but I will entertain a few questions. I'd like to get the jump on this story. I don't want any of them formulating their own survival theories."

Rupert nodded and moved to the other side of the luxurious cabin to set to the task of putting in a call to the White House press secretary. As he waited for the call to be patched through he instructed Caroline's personal secretary to join her in preparation for dictation.

As Caroline dictated some long-overdue correspondence, a part of her remained focused on her husband's face. There was one scar starting at his right temple and slashing down his jaw, but otherwise his face was unmarred. She frowned as she studied him. He looked younger somehow. Or perhaps she simply felt older. God knew she'd aged a decade in the past three months.

She assumed he had burned his hands attempting to free himself from the wreckage. At the hospital as he'd dressed in the clothes Rupert had kindly thought to bring along, she had noticed a number of scars on Justin's back as well. His hair was a little longer than before but not much else had changed.

And still, everything felt different. She imagined that it was her own guilt intruding. Or maybe some part of her was still convinced this was only a dream and that she would wake up to that same ugly reality any moment.

But it wasn't a dream. He was alive. She had a second chance…at everything.

The plane abruptly dipped sending papers flying. Her secretary barely caught the laptop in time. Caroline's gaze collided with Rupert's. His reflected the same question as hers. What now?

Her stomach dropped to her feet as the nose of the plane dropped again then jerked upward.

"What the hell is going on?" Rupert shouted as he got to his feet to investigate.

Agent Howard Copeland appeared seemingly out of nowhere.

"What's happening up there?" Rupert demanded, slanting a look toward the cockpit.

"Please fasten your seat belt, Madam President,"

Copeland said to Caroline. "Yours as well, ma'am," he said to the secretary before bothering with Rupert's demand. "Please, sir," he said then, his tone calm but firm, "keep your seat and buckle up. You'll be safer that way."

Rupert didn't appear appeased, but he followed the agent's instructions. The rest of the security detail was moving into place around Caroline, whispering among themselves and making the necessary preparations.

"What's going on, Agent Copeland?" Caroline asked, maintaining a professional tone despite the quaking going on inside her.

The agent looked directly at her then and she saw the fleeting glimmer of fear in his eyes. "Everything is fine, Madam President," he said then forced a dim smile. "We're having some engine trouble, but we'll be fine."

Caroline knew it was a lie.

Her gaze sought her husband. Those clear blue eyes were open now and staring back at her with an intensity that sent a new kind of shiver over her skin.

He didn't have to say a word.

He knew.

He had experienced this same moment once before.

They were going to crash.

Chapter Three

Lockdown
San Antonio, Texas

They were alive.

Caroline closed her eyes and thought about just how close they had come to crashing. If not for the expertise of the captain and his co-pilot, things would have turned out very differently.

The captain had managed a hard landing at a San Antonio airstrip. Rescue personnel as well as local law-enforcement and state police had been on hand for the landing. The entire presidential entourage had been quickly transported to the San Antonio police department where the whole building went into lockdown mode. There wasn't a U.S. Marshal or FBI agent for a hundred miles who hadn't shown up to help out with the Code Red emergency.

A military detail from nearby Fort Sam Houston had arrived posthaste. Caroline felt completely secure despite still being shaken by the whole event. She could only imagine how Justin felt after what he'd been through already. His seemingly calm exterior surprised her. But then again, he had no memory of the crash. Perhaps that was a blessing under the circumstances.

Justin had never been a particularly courageous man. A good·man. An ambitious man. But not uncommonly brave. That he held his composure so well during the crisis felt…odd. Giving him grace, Dr. Hernandez had warned her that he was not the same man she'd last seen before he'd departed on that ill-fated journey to Brazil. She'd spoken to him once during his three-day business trip to Rio De Janeiro. The conversation had been clipped, his tone distant. Then she hadn't heard from him again. He and the others, including one Secret Service agent, had boarded the company jet for the return trip, not to be heard from again. Until now.

"President Winters, are you certain I can't get you some more coffee or a soft drink?" Chief of Police Parnell asked again. "The same goes for anyone else," he said to the room at large.

When Caroline declined, Agent Copeland, as well as the rest of the security detail, followed suit. Rupert and Justin did the same. There were times when she felt certain those around her went without what they really wanted so as not to react differently from her.

"Pizza would be good," she suggested on second thought, knowing none of her people had bothered with lunch and the dinner hour was looming. "Can we get something delivered?"

"Why, yes, ma'am." The chief literally beamed. At

last he had something to do. She could see the excitement in his eyes. "Any particular kind? Soft drinks too?"

A mere forty-five minutes later, large pizzas with the works and cold soft drinks had been served all around. The pizza delivery boy had arrived with the goods as well as a disposable camera in hopes of getting his picture taken with the president. When security pressed the issue the chief admitted that the young man was his nephew. A collective sigh of relief flowed over the room and for no other reason than she felt the need to give the chief a break, Caroline agreed to the picture—much to Rupert's dismay.

When the group was occupied with devouring the warm pizza, Caroline used the moment of quiet to study Justin again. His movements, his mannerisms were the same. Deliberate, precise. If she had to pinpoint one characteristic that was purely Justin it would be his careful deliberation of his every word and deed. He rarely spoke or moved out of turn. That had not changed. Funny, she mused, how some things were different, like his voice and the lack of sparkle in his eyes, while other things stayed exactly the same. She imagined his voice was rusty from the months of disuse while in a coma.

She wanted a full physical and mental evaluation ASAP.

It wasn't that she doubted the competence of the physician in Mexico City, but Justin's personal physician knew his history. Knew him. He would more quickly pick up on anything that proved out of sync.

"Are you holding up all right?" she asked him when

he caught her staring at him. She shivered before she could catch herself, startled once more by the impact of his eyes. That cool distance cut right through her.

"I'm fine now," he said in that voice that sounded too deep and too gravelly. "And you?"

Was she okay? On one level she was great. Justin was alive. She thanked God yet again for the miracle. But things were off somehow. She felt disconnected in ways she couldn't quite label.

"I'm all right." She smiled warmly at him. "Shaken, but all right."

He returned her smile and it was the same lopsided expression he'd flashed her hundreds of times before. Her pulse reacted in a way that it hadn't in a very long time. What made it feel different now?

Maybe she was simply functioning on the adrenaline rush of outright panic and its inescapable drain. A lot had happened the past few days. The trouble with Redmond and her Cabinet. Learning that Justin was alive and then the near-crash, it was all catching up to her now.

Sleep was the answer. She needed to rest her mind.

Before she had time to analyze the situation further, a second security detail arrived, along with new pilots who would fly Caroline, Justin and Rupert to Andrews Air Force Base. The remainder of the group would follow on a civilian airliner.

Incredibly her press secretary stormed into the conference room amid the fresh lot of Secret Service personnel.

"Aaron?" She tried to read what was behind his grave

expression as he approached but proved unsuccessful. "You needn't have come all this way."

And he wouldn't have, she knew, unless something was wrong.

Aaron Miller, along with Greg Levitt, the agent no doubt in charge of the new arrivals, ushered Caroline and Rupert to a quiet corner of the room. "We have some new intelligence that you're going to want to hear, Madam President."

Rupert frowned. Caroline felt the same creases in her expression. "What kind of intelligence?" Rupert asked.

"Madam President," Levitt said, derailing anything she would have asked, "we received a threat on your life at the same time the plane started to give the pilot trouble."

The implications of that statement slammed into her hard. "You're certain of that?" She had to ask, though she knew this discussion would not be happening otherwise.

"Yes, ma'am," Levitt assured her, "we are. Shortly after we learned that Air Force One had managed a safe landing, we received another threat."

"Whoever is behind this may know where we are," Rupert said quickly, his voice taking on an urgency that unsettled Caroline more so than anything Levitt could have said.

"What is your recommendation?" she asked the deliverer of the bad news. Copeland had started in their direction. He would have gotten a heads-up on this already. Since he hadn't mentioned it to her, she assumed the news had come only moments before Levitt's arrival.

"We're going to take you to a safe location for the moment, Madam President, then we'll go from there."

Caroline shook her head. No. This was what the terrorists behind this act wanted. "I see no reason to treat this threat any differently than any other. We'll go back to the White House as scheduled."

Levitt deferred to Copeland with a covert look that spoke volumes. A sinking feeling dragged at Caroline's stomach.

"Ma'am," Copeland began somberly, "This isn't just any threat. Whoever made this threat got to Air Force One. The Captain has already zeroed in on the problem. There was an electronic device planted to interfere with the plane's fuel system. Whoever put it there never intended for the plane to actually go down, it was simply a warning. A timer on the device only permitted it to be operational for a few minutes. Just long enough for us to have to make an emergency landing."

"This threat has to be coming from the inside, ma'am," Levitt continued. "No one else knew your precise agenda. No one else could have gotten to the plane."

Redmond was the first name that came to mind but Caroline held her tongue. That plummeting sensation that had started in her stomach was spiraling upward, turning her worry into outright fury. First the bizarre calls and the note, then the near-crash…now this.

For the first time since she'd learned that Justin was alive she suddenly wondered about the calls and the note. Had someone at the hospital figured out who he was and decided to play some sick game? She rejected that theory. Whoever had made those calls had known the right number to call, hadn't gone through the switchboard.

Her gaze sought and found Justin where he sat with his eyes closed, resting, weary from it all. Could he have made those calls? Unknowingly, of course. The doctor had insisted he'd been in a coma the whole time. Had he acted out the calls for help while lost in that zone between sleeping and waking? He might not even know he'd made the calls. Whether or not the calls came from the hospital would be easy to verify. And yet the White House lines showed no unidentified incoming calls. Nothing. No indication whatsoever that she had received any such calls.

Caroline looked to Rupert. "What's your assessment of the situation, Mr. Downy?" It wasn't that she didn't trust her own instincts, but she wanted a second opinion.

"Let's not take any chances, Madam President. You'd already committed to some time off," Rupert offered frankly. "Aaron can handle the press conference. We'll let the people know that Justin is alive and that you're taking some time with him. Meanwhile we'll work on getting to the bottom of…this situation."

No one wanted to say out loud the truth that sat like a stone on her chest. A mole had gotten close enough to have her agenda on short notice…to have access to her means of transportation.

Caroline looked around the room with as much denial as disbelief. It could be anyone. Firming her resolve, her gaze landed back on Levitt. She trusted the people in this room. There had to be another explanation. She would give them three days to complete their assessment then she was getting back to her life…to her duties.

"You have seventy-two hours," she said, her tone leaving no room for discussion. "I'll take a short hiatus in a safe location and manage any situation that arises from there. But no more. Seventy-two hours only. Then I'm returning to the White House whether you've found the traitor or not." Another little voice inside her wanted to shout Redmond's name. But she didn't have to do that. Levitt and Copeland were both well aware of the animosity between their president and vice president. Redmond would be the first suspect on their list. "On Monday evening I have that graduation. I will be there."

Rupert groaned. "Madam President, we need to—"

"My mind is made up," she cut him off. "I'm not going to play dead for these people. We should keep this out of the media," she said with that thought. "No one needs to know. The engine malfunctioned today. End of story. Let's not give these bastards the satisfaction of seeing their work on the national news."

Aaron nodded. "Done. I'll issue that statement as well as the news about Justin at the same time, Madam President."

Caroline watched Justin for a moment while Rupert and the two agents carried on with the discussion. He was so very still. And yet there was an energy about him. Something she'd never noticed before. Odd.

What other changes, she suddenly wondered, had his up close encounter with death inspired?

Three days of quiet with little or no distraction. She

imagined that she would know the answer to that question very soon. The real question was, was she ready for the answer? She wondered vaguely why running a country at times felt easier than the balancing act of marriage.

Safe House
Classified Location

As THE SUV rolled up the long drive, Cain surveyed the dark setting. It was almost midnight now. They'd landed at Andrews Air Force Base and then taken ground transportation from there. The president's senior advisor and press secretary had loaded into a decoy vehicle to draw the press away from the base. The diversion had worked like a charm. Minutes after the last of the paparazzi had left, the vehicle he and Caroline occupied had moved through the gate.

The security detail was lighter than Cain had expected. Only six men, but, according to Caroline, they were the best. He wasn't worried, though he hadn't allowed her to see his level of comfort.

As they neared their destination now, he watched her through the darkness. The dim lights from the dash of the vehicle spared little illumination in the back seat but Cain had excellent night vision. Like a cat, he mused.

She was more attractive than the pictures and videos he'd seen. Perhaps it was the vulnerability he sensed in her now that softened her usual tough edge. Caroline Winters was an independent woman, one who was intimidated by little if anything at all. Yet something had managed to get under her skin. Cain suspected it was far more than the current threat to her life, which had been staged for this very purpose.

Center needed her out of the limelight, hidden away until the real threat could be assessed. Whoever intended to remove her from office would be far more subtle than today's showy display.

Cain's mission was to protect her at all costs while Center ferreted out the force behind the intelligence they had recently uncovered. The only way to be completely sure of her safety and, at the same time, leave her open for approach was to do exactly as they had.

The Lazarus Mission.

The resurrection of her dead husband had been the only way to get someone close to her without anyone suspecting just who would be protecting her. Complete secrecy was essential. When the mission was complete her husband would disappear once more. Only this time he would stay dead.

A small two-story home came into view beyond the headlights. Picket fence, lots of flowering shrubs. It looked like a modern cottage set deep in the woods in a world all its own.

Only there were a few added precautions for security's sake. An eight-foot hot-wired fence enclosed the ten acres surrounding the small, harmless-looking house. Trip sensors were scattered over the grounds extending for a thousand feet around the house. Every imaginable precaution had been taken inside the home as well. Bulletproof glass in the windows. Full brick exterior. The materials the home had been constructed of were fire-resistant. The only way anyone would get to her inside this house was to drop a bomb on it.

And since the air space around it was closely monitored, that wasn't going to happen without advance warning.

She would be safe here.

Cain's presence would simply ensure that the other humans around her stayed on the right side. He would protect her from anyone with whom she came into contact.

If the traitor had burrowed in amid her own staffers, he or she would find a way to show up here.

Cain would be ready.

He'd never failed in a mission.

CAROLINE HAD HEARD of this place. The ultimate in "safe houses." It had been created to protect political refugees who held information the United States wanted. Their safety could be guaranteed while they lived in luxurious—however out-of-the-way—comfort.

"Everything you and Mr. Winters will need has been provided, Madam President," Agent Levitt said. "There are eight men on site already. We'll have six on duty around the clock. Our shifts will be twelve on/twelve off."

She nodded. "Excellent. That'll be all, Agent Levitt."

With the final mini-briefing out of the way, Caroline and Justin were left in privacy. Only two agents would actually be inside the house. Levitt or Copeland and one more. The others would man the grounds, which included a fully furnished and stocked guest house in the rear.

Caroline headed up the stairs. There were two bedrooms, one smaller bedroom and a generous room with an en suite dressing area and bath. Downstairs there was a roomy den, an office with conference table, a dining room and state-of-the-art kitchen. Another smaller office was tucked away near the den.

Tomorrow morning Caroline intended to have her usual morning briefing with her staff, as well as the usual intelligence updates from the FBI, CIA and NSA. Activities in the Middle East required her near-constant attention, despite the recent strides toward peace in the area. Fuel prices had finally stabilized, but many constituents as well as lobbyists were still up in arms with the costs continuing to hover above what they had been in the early part of the former administration. She had her work cut out for her in those two arenas. There was no reason for her to be uninformed during this time or to rely on secondhand information. Satellite communications ensured she could reach out and touch anyone she needed to, anytime, anyplace, with the highest level of security.

"Are you tired?" she asked Justin when they'd entered the lovely suite. She felt suddenly nervous in this room with him. As if they hadn't been married for more than five years. As if the bed were far too intimate an object to share.

"Yes," he said in answer though she saw no physical indication that he felt weary. But he must. He'd been hospitalized for months. In a coma most of that time. He must be exhausted just moving about.

She managed an understanding smile. "Why don't you go ahead and stretch out? I think I'll have a long soak in the tub." She craned her neck from side to side and grimaced at the tight muscles. "I'm beat."

Not waiting for a comment, she crossed to the dressing room and the walk-in closet there. The closet held several days' attire for both her and Justin. Everything had been taken care of before their arrival. She rummaged around until she found a suitable nightgown, then entered the elegant bath, closing the door behind her.

As the hot water filled the tub, she tried to reason out the conflicting feelings that had plagued her since hearing that Justin was alive. She closed her eyes and braced her hands on the marble topped vanity. Relief and gratitude that he was alive surged through her all over again. There was no denying those emotions.

She opened her eyes and stared at her reflection in the mirror. But where did they go from here?

Her entire marriage to Justin had been a lie. An ache went through her at the admission. She rarely allowed herself to consider their union in those terms. But it was true. They had known each other since high school, had dated during her last year in law school but the relationship had never been serious. Then as she took office in the Senate, their paths had crossed once more. This time she'd fallen completely for him. He'd tried to discourage her pursuit. But she'd been thirty-two and completely ready for a commitment. She had so loved Justin.

He'd loved her too. She'd known it with every fiber of her being. And though they had never been intimate he'd insisted that he believed strongly in saving sex for the marriage bed. They'd continued in that manner for a time. Her wanting the big white wedding, him wanting to give the relationship more time—to be absolutely certain it was what they both wanted. In retrospect, she should have seen what was coming.

Then Rupert approached her about running for president. The next election was four years away, which gave her plenty of time to build a running platform. There were others he'd told her who wanted to see a woman in the Oval Office as well. Powerful men who could make it happen.

Caroline hadn't actually believed the dream would come to fruition, but she had secretly wanted it. Had ever since her father's failed bid for the White House. If she could make it, she could carry on with his plans. Point this great nation in the right direction. Make sure all Americans had the proper health care and that social security was safe for the aging population. There was so much she could do.

So she'd gone for it, never once looking back. Justin had popped the question and she'd gotten that big, beautiful wedding to boot.

Little had she known it would come with a high price. Her new husband loved her, that much had been true. But he had not been able to bring himself to make love to her. Caroline had at first been certain it was her. There was something wrong with her. She was too domineering, too confident, had too high a profile in society. All those things together turned off her sensitive husband.

That had to be the answer. Then she'd gone through the scenario that perhaps he was gay and had never admitted the truth to himself. That he'd hoped marrying her would kick his resistant libido into action. But that apparently hadn't been so either.

Justin had never confessed to being gay and had not once given her any reason to suspect he was. Nor had he ever touched her intimately. Oh, they had kissed, mostly for the sake of the cameras and the watchful eyes all around them. But that was as far as it had gone.

Living with Justin was like living with a brother or sister. It was utterly asexual. There was not a spark of chemistry between them, not a glimmer of desire.

Caroline slipped into the neck-deep water of the whirlpool tub and allowed the heat to soothe her aching muscles, allowed it to clear her mind. It felt so good. Like the protective walls of a mother's womb.

For maybe a minute the distraction worked, then her thoughts returned exactly to where she'd left off.

She had reviewed their years of courtship over and over, relived in her mind every kiss, every touch. She'd felt the sparks, had experienced the desire. But, in looking back, she'd realized that it had all been one sided. She had been attracted to him. She had desired him. He was always the one who held back…who pushed her away when she got too close.

And deep down maybe a part of her had needed Justin on any level. She'd lost her father that last year of law school. Justin had been there for her. His strength had supported her so many times.

A soul-deep sigh slipped past her lips. Perhaps she had been in love with the strength he offered, with the father figure he represented. This wasn't entirely his fault. She had pursued him more so than the other way around.

Yet, Justin was not innocent in this mess. He had withheld the truth from her. Lied. There was no way to make it pretty. By not admitting his lack of sexual attraction to her he had, in fact, lied. Even worse, when he'd learned that she would make a bid for the ultimate position of power, he'd let himself get carried away with the frenzy. Rupert had suggested that a wedding would facilitate her efforts to gain the highest office in the land. Justin had been all too ready to claim the role of husband to the future president.

That had been the source of their heated exchange the day he'd left for Brazil. She'd grown weary of the pretense. She was thirty-seven years old. The opportunity to have a child was quickly passing her by. She wanted a child. She could live without a husband to hold her each night. At least she had for five long years. But the idea of living the rest of her life without having held her child in her arms, without giving birth, was simply more than she could bear. Even if she was the president, she was still a woman.

On that fateful morning three months ago, she had given him an ultimatum. Fulfill her wish for a child or call it quits. She had nearly four years to smooth over a presidential divorce with the voters. It was a chance she felt compelled to take. He had until he returned from Brazil to make his decision.

Then his plane had gone down.

And she had been left to live with her harsh, self-serving words echoing in her ears.

Forcing the painful memories away, she leaned forward and turned on the tap again to add a little more hot water.

The door opened, jerking her attention in that direction and automatically sending her arm over her naked breasts. She twisted the knob, shutting off the water with her free hand.

Justin, wearing pajama pants, his chest bare, strode across the room without slowing once. He settled on the edge of the tub and smiled down at her.

"I thought maybe I could rub those tense shoulders now that you've soaked awhile."

His voice sounded softer, almost velvety. It shivered over her senses like silk skimming her naked flesh.

Without waiting for her response since she'd clearly turned mute in the last three seconds, he placed those strong, scarred hands on her shoulders and squeezed. His thumbs pressed into her at just the right pressure points while those fingers rolled and kneaded her tense muscles.

"Feel good?" he murmured.

Her entire body reacted to both his touch and his voice. "Yes," she confessed, whispered.

He leaned down, put his mouth close to her ear. "Just relax. I want to do this for you." He kissed the spot just beneath her earlobe and fire shot straight to her loins. The gasp that escaped her mouth echoed loudly in the room. "I've missed you," he murmured.

An unexpected heat roared through her. She wanted to question him. To demand of him what he thought he was doing. But she couldn't speak; she could only react to the touch of those rough hands…to the surprising, yet pleasant chemistry of his body so near to hers.

He tortured her like that for more than half an hour. By the time he stopped she wanted to grab him and pull him into the water with her.

But this was Justin.

He didn't want to make love to her.

He didn't want her that way.

He'd never wanted her that way.

His lips pressed to her temple as his hands grew still on her skin. "I'll draw back the covers and pour us a glass of wine." He stood, crossed the room, and closed the door behind him, her gaze following every subtle shift of male muscle as he moved.

Her breasts felt heavy and achy. Her sex tingled and throbbed in a way that startled her. It had been so long since she'd felt like this…since she'd known desire. Her body ached for release. How long had it been? So long she'd even stopped pleasuring herself, had given up on a sex life entirely—told herself it didn't matter.

But now her body strummed with need, ached with want. Easing back down into the water, Caroline slid her fingers to that needy place and stroked. It only took a moment and then much-needed release exploded inside her, making her cry out in hollow longing. It had been so very long.

She curled up in the water, wrapped her arms around

her knees as the final waves of release rippled through her. So long.

How could she be the most powerful woman on earth and still be reduced to a quivering mass by a man who'd refused to touch her for more than five years?

Chapter Four

72 Hours Remaining

Caroline watched the television as Aaron Miller, her press secretary, did a stellar job of dodging questions while he conducted the press conference announcing Justin's survival. She knew without having to be told by those keeping their fingers on the pulse of the ratings and viewer polls that two out of every three Americans between the ages of twenty-five and eighty-five would be watching this breaking news story.

Justin Winters, husband of President Caroline Winters, was alive. His incredible return was being cited as a "Resurrection from the Dead" by the *Post* and various others in the media circus.

Caroline closed her eyes and blocked out the images…the sound of Aaron's carefully modulated tone and cautiously worded statements. Her mind kept replaying the way her husband had touched her last night. She couldn't remember the last time he'd offered to rub her tense muscles or provide any physical comfort to her in any way. That he'd slept spooned against her throughout the entire night still shook her to the very core of her being.

It had taken hours for her to get to sleep as her body betrayed her, memorizing every contour of his pressed so intimately next to hers. One strong arm had rested firmly around her waist as if he feared she might somehow disappear during the night.

She shook her head and forced her attention back on the evolving events on the screen. She tried to tell herself it was the miraculous survival—his defiance of death—that made him cling to her. Or even that the bed was smaller, which left him no choice but to nestle close. But the bed was the same California king-size as the one in their bedroom at the White House. And Justin had always been far too practical and levelheaded to allow a mere thing like thwarting death to send him over the edge of control.

Then again, maybe the accident had changed him more than she'd anticipated. The doctors had warned that he might not be the same. Unable to help herself she sneaked a glance in his direction. On the other side of the comfortable office, relaxed in a thickly upholstered chair with his long legs stretched out on a matching ottoman, his full attention appeared to be glued to the book in his hand. He insisted on staying close to her. Another unsettling deviation from the norm. The only time they'd spent apart thus far today was when she'd attended the daily briefings via SATCOM.

Though he certainly stayed right by her side while

under the scrutiny of others, especially the media, at home—behind closed doors—they rarely shared anything other than meals. That wasn't entirely true. They still shared a good laugh over dinner now and then and stories about their respective days. It wasn't fair to paint the man with the same brush that she painted the husband. Justin was a good man, but he failed miserably as a husband.

The press conference ended and Caroline felt immensely relieved. Rupert had insisted that she give them seventy-two hours starting this morning rather than yesterday and she had reluctantly agreed. Admittedly she needed time to adjust to her husband's return, to prepare herself for facing the questions that would linger for weeks, and to give security the chance to assess the newest threat to her life.

She rubbed her eyes and braced her elbows on the desk and considered this morning's briefings. The CIA had garnered more intelligence related to the unrest churning in South America. The trouble in Colombia was rapidly turning the tide of worry in that direction and away from the perpetually smoldering situation in the Middle East. She had already authorized a problem-solving delegation headed by Secretary of State Samuel Hall, which was negotiating with the rebels and the Colombian government even now in hopes of settling the mushrooming trouble. Civil unrest and rebel uprising were nothing new to Colombia, but what was new was the spilling over of that antagonism to surrounding countries. Sides were being taken, real trouble appeared on the horizon.

If the U.S. didn't play peacemaker, who would? That undeniable and heavy burden fell solidly on her shoulders. She didn't really have time for personal affairs. She damn sure didn't have time to hide out like this. Still, she wasn't stupid enough to thumb her nose at a threat this serious. To protect herself was to protect the country.

Redmond. If she found out that he had anything to do with the threat to assassinate her, she would see that he faced the fullest possible punishment for his actions. How could she not have recognized that the man thrived on greed? She'd been so blind to his machinations. But she had his number now. He'd better watch his step or he would end up on the wrong side of a treason charge.

His cronies within the ranks on Capitol Hill wouldn't be able to save him if it came to that. A part of her hoped it didn't. She prayed her gut instinct on the matter was wrong. But she had a bad feeling she was right. Someone or some group had gotten to him. It hadn't started out this way. She'd sensed in him the same goals as her own in the beginning. But soon after inauguration things had changed. Or maybe she simply wanted to believe that. Maybe he'd simply fooled her as Rupert suggested.

When her husband had disappeared things had only gotten worse. It was as if he'd used the opportunity to take advantage of her vulnerability. He'd even gone so far as to allow himself to be quoted that hers was a unique situation in the history of the nation, referring to her female emotions.

Her teeth clenched hard. Whatever schemes he'd

hatched, he would not win. She intended to fight…intended to win.

No one was going to get in her way.

A shiver of awareness went through her and her gaze instantly shifted to Justin.

He was watching her. His gaze so intent she shivered again. A ping of vulnerability rippled along every nerve ending as if he'd read her mind.

"Aaron did a good job," he offered with a kind smile as he set aside his book. "He said all the right things." Justin settled his feet on the floor and braced his elbows on his spread knees. "Rupert told me the whole nation wept for your loss when they thought I was dead. I'm sure they're cheering for you now. They love you, Caroline. Whatever decisions you make will be the right ones."

She managed a wan smile. "Thank you, Justin. Your support means a great deal to me." She looked away a moment before meeting his gaze once more. "I am glad you're back. I…" Swallowing hard she wondered how she could say the rest. "After the way we left things, the idea that I would never be able to make it right was nearly more than I could bear." She braced against the inevitable emotions that attempted to surface. They hadn't talked about that last morning…the things she'd said. Was he merely sparing her feelings?

He pushed to his feet and moved toward her. Again she found herself mesmerized by the way he moved. It wasn't that his walk was different…not really. It was more the smooth, predatory nature of it that simply hadn't been there before. She shook herself. Or maybe she was imagining the whole thing. He crouched beside her chair and took her hand in his.

"I don't remember much about that day or the ones that followed. I can almost remember wandering aimlessly or maybe I can't remember it at all. The fleeting memories could merely be connected to what the medical staff told me when I finally came out of the coma," he confessed, his face a study in regret. "But I do know that I've spent every waking moment since thinking about you and how much I missed you. Whatever went wrong before, I want to make it right."

What was he saying? That he was prepared to be a real husband to her? Children? Her heart leapt at the possibility. But could she trust this new attitude to stick? What if he reverted back to his old ways as he healed completely over time?

She stared at the big hand engulfing hers. "I'll have to think about this, Justin," she said, her gaze moving up to meet his. The intensity there made her quiver. He looked so sincere, so needy. But was that the real motivation behind this change of heart? His needs. Had he suddenly learned the fragility of life and decided to grab on with both hands whether he really wanted her or not?

He brushed a soft kiss to her cheek. The surge of desire the chaste act prompted made her breath catch in her throat.

"Take all the time you need. I'll be waiting."

He left the room...left her to struggle with that challenge. For the first time in all these years, he wanted her.

Was willing to give her, it seemed, all that she wanted in a marriage. In a husband.

But was it too little too late?

Could she forget the past and be happy?

Caroline cradled her head in her hands and tried to think rationally. This was what she'd wanted. What she'd demanded. Why the second thoughts?

And then she knew.

For the first time since the early days of their marriage, she wanted desperately for it to be true. She wanted Justin to want her simply for her with no other motivation…such as his continued residency at the White House.

CAIN WATCHED from the dining room as Caroline discussed various issues with her senior advisor in the living room. Rupert had arrived a couple of hours after the press briefing and just in time for lunch. Cain cocked his head and studied the woman who was president.

She was strong, confident, extremely intelligent. Right now she felt fury at her vice president for what she called his indifferent treatment of her personal staff back at the White House. This morning, shortly after the press conference Aaron Miller had held, her secretary had mentioned an incident involving Vice President Redmond that infuriated Caroline. Rupert worked hard to smooth over the incident. Cain hadn't decided just yet whether the man was friend or foe. He appeared to have Caroline's best interests at heart and she certainly seemed to trust him.

Bottom line, in the scheme of things Rupert had the most access to the president. He could be the one working the hardest against her. Had the culprit been her husband, the issue would be moot since he was dead. The world had watched the official search teams scramble to find survivors or remains via one news network after the other, but it had been Center's team that was successful. Using technology unavailable to the rest of the planet as of yet, Center had quickly located part of Justin Winters' remains, allowing Cain to wear the gold band that represented the marriage between him and Caroline. Though most of the items recovered from the wreckage were damaged beyond any sort of salvaging, Center had thoroughly analyzed every bit

They had learned from another source that Justin Winters had met with a South American connection that could be related to the Concern, an enemy of the United States, Center in particular. But that lead had not been confirmed. No one even knew of the possible connection other than Director O'Riley and Cain himself. O'Riley had every reason to believe that the dead husband held no predominant position in the scheme of things. He might simply have been a pawn used to bring pain into Caroline's life.

Like most humans, she had suffered greatly over the loss. Yet she had held up exceedingly well. Cain felt reasonably certain that he had discovered why.

He had studied Caroline's life as well as Justin's. Nothing in their history indicated they had anything other than a happy marriage. In every image he'd viewed, from old news clips to magazines and newspapers, the couple had appeared to be happily married. But they weren't. When he'd touched her last night she'd stiffened, shown surprise at the move. She'd resisted lying so close to him in bed last night, but he'd forced the issue. When he'd kissed her cheek this morning she'd gasped. She was startled by the intimacy of his actions. Startled and angered on some level.

It didn't add up. Though he had never been involved in that sort of relationship, he understood perfectly how the concept of marriage worked. And this one clearly hadn't.

Whatever problems had plagued the two, he had to work past them. He needed her to trust him—in every way, on every level. That wasn't going to happen without the bond of physical intimacy. He'd anticipated the need to explain away any differences she noted in his anatomy or his skill as a lovemaking partner. Now he doubted the need. Judging by her rush toward physical release as he'd massaged her shoulders and then the subsequent self-stimulation after he'd left the room, Cain concluded that sexual intimacy had not existed in this marriage for quite sometime.

This woman intrigued him. She appeared so strong, so invincible, and yet she had no control over the human closest to her…her husband. Her physical needs went unfulfilled. And she allowed it. Something stirred deep inside Cain. An attraction of some sort that contained no logical motivation or foundation. No human had ever moved him. Perhaps, he reconsidered, that once, in a former mission, when he'd allowed the Archer woman to live his peer Adam had reached him on some level. But the events of that mission had been more about trust than anything else. There had been no true emotional basis other than simple logic. Adam had known the woman better than him, why not trust his instincts?

Perhaps, Cain decided, the physical relationship in this case was what intrigued him. He was well versed in the art of copulation. Acting out the steps would not be difficult. He'd passed all the compatibility tests required. This certainly wasn't the first time he'd been thrust into a setting that required interaction with other humans. All Enforcers, though housed on Center away from the real world, were highly trained in intra-personal relationships. He'd lived for weeks at a time away from Center to sharpen his ability to fit into the social network of society. He watched the news, read all the right newspapers and journals.

But this was different.

He felt some vague connection to this woman he had never felt before. A part of him considered it to be a good thing, a way to gain trust more quickly. But another part of him sensed danger. He should not allow this connection to grow or strengthen in any way.

His mission was to keep her alive at all costs. To gain her trust by any means necessary.

No other factor played into the scenario. He had to keep that foremost in his mind.

Emotional vulnerability was not a part of his makeup. Whatever illogical reaction this woman stirred in him, it had no emotional basis. Perhaps it was simple chemistry. He understood the theory, though he had certainly never experienced it.

Cain refocused on the conversation going on in the living room, pushing all else aside. Clearly, Caroline was not happy with the outcome.

"End of discussion, Rupert. I did not sign that letter and, besides, I wrote it before." She stabbed a finger in her senior advisor's direction. "At your urging, I might add. You tell Redmond that just because a copy of it ended up in his hands and he got a glimpse of my pain doesn't mean I'll allow him to act upon it. In case he's forgotten, my decision is the only one that counts."

Rupert nodded. "Very well, Madam President."

She exited the room and headed up the stairs. Cain watched her go until she was out of sight then shifted his gaze to the man left in the wake of her less-than-pleasant departure. Rupert looked downtrodden. But all that she'd said was true. Though he might care deeply for Caroline, his counsel had apparently worsened an already seriously screwed-up situation. Was he working for her or her enemies?

Only time would tell.

When he'd made some innocuous parting remark to the agent stationed at the front door, Rupert left considerably less happily than he'd arrived. Cain watched through the front window as he was driven away. Security wouldn't allow for his coming straight here. He'd had to rendezvous with Agent Levitt who'd taken him on a route designed to lose all tails before bringing him to the safe-house location. If word of the president's whereabouts was leaked within the ranks of her staff, pinpointing the traitor would be relatively simple since only a chosen few knew the location and anyone else who showed up would be out of place.

Cain topped the second-story landing and strode toward the room where Caroline had no doubt taken refuge. She was angry and needed to think. She didn't like any of this. He read her quite well already. Sensed a number of disturbing anxieties tugging at her. Caroline Winters desperately needed to count on someone who seemingly had no motivation for wanting to see her professional weakness. Someone like a husband.

Only she didn't trust her husband.

That was something Cain was going to have to earn.

She burst through the bedroom door just as he reached it.

Startled, she glared up at him. "I'm going for a run."

Security wouldn't like any sudden changes to the routine, but the determination she emitted left little doubt that changing her mind would entail nothing less than physically restraining her.

"That's a good idea." He squeezed her arm. "We could both use an outlet about now."

She blinked, surprised all over again. "You don't... you might not be well enough to—"

"I'm fine," he countered before she could say more. "The doctors ensured my muscles were stimulated by therapists as well as by electrical impulse while I was in the coma. It didn't leave me in such bad shape." He smiled and moved a few inches closer. "Do you doubt my ability to keep up with you?"

She stared into his eyes until he felt her resistance give, then she shook her head. "Suit yourself. I'll be warming up downstairs."

Pulling her arm loose from his hold she moved away from him, then stalked off toward the stairs. She didn't like his ability to divert her determination. He'd have to be careful that the resentment didn't grow more quickly than the desire.

He knew precisely what he had to do next.

LEVITT HAD BLOWN a fuse when she'd first announced that she intended to take another run beyond the regular morning routine without first allowing him time to prepare for the unscheduled event, but Caroline had refused to relent. By the time she'd convinced the agent that she would not be swayed from her decision, Justin had joined her in the downstairs entry hall. His constant presence did little to alleviate her irritation. She felt immediately contrite at the thought.

He'd almost died, was damned lucky to be alive. How could she resent his need to stay close to her? Whether motivated by fate or design, he appeared determined to make things right between them. The one worry that kept Caroline from jumping into his arms and shouting her thanks to the very heavens was that he might get over it. That it was only temporary. What if he woke up a few weeks from now and realized the truth about them?

That he'd never wanted her like that. That he actually felt no sexual preference one way or another. She'd asked, not making any bones about it. She remembered the conversation as if it had taken place just yesterday. *Just tell me the truth, Justin. Are you gay?*

He'd insisted that her question was unfounded. He simply lacked any sexual ambition one way or another. She'd even urged him to seek medical help or counseling to no avail. He would not discuss the issue. He didn't want her in that way; he didn't want anyone. Justin Winters was happy simply to be. He loved life, loved her. He just didn't want to have a sexual relationship with her. The whole idea had gone against the grain.

God had created man and woman to procreate. To bond sexually. Yet, Justin felt no such need. No such desire. Period.

Leaving her empty.

She pushed onward, her feet pounding against the ground as she circled the property yet again. She'd been at it for more than thirty minutes but it wasn't nearly enough. She refused even to glance at him. He'd managed to keep up with her every step of the way. His stamina, considering his recent hospital stay, surprised her. Surprised her even without the knowledge that he'd very nearly died a few months ago. Justin had worked out the requisite three times per week, but he'd never been a diehard runner. He had only run with her a couple of times to play up their "togetherness" for the media.

That he scarcely broke a sweat and certainly wasn't breathing hard when she was perspiring like crazy and panting like a dog who'd gone too long without water made her all the more furious.

Damn him.

A man who'd only recently survived a catastrophic plane crash should scarcely be able to walk, much less run.

She rubbed the sweat from her eyes with the back of her hand and resisted the urge to shake her head. She was jealous of his physical stamina. Jealous! How ridiculous was that? She should be damned thankful he was alive and what was she doing? Whining over his ability to outlast her on the track.

Not once in her life had she known herself to be so self-absorbed. What was happening to her? First she was imagining that she was hearing his voice and receiving a letter from him; now she was resenting his very existence?

Maybe she was losing her grip on reality. Maybe she should have signed that letter invoking the Twenty-Fifth. She sure as hell was second-guessing herself a lot lately. Not a good thing in a commander in chief.

"Wait!"

She stopped at the abrupt word. Justin, bent at the waist, hands resting on his thighs, gasped for breath. "I'm sorry. I don't think I can go on any longer."

The four-man security detail fell into strategic positions around their location, at once taking advantage of the most effective protection plan and giving their principals some measure of privacy to talk.

All the mean-spirited thoughts she'd just had twisted in her gut like a cache of double-edged swords.

"Are you all right?" She hurried to him, hesitantly placing her hand on one massive shoulder. The physical reaction was immediate and intense, like an explosion of heat soaring through her veins.

He nodded, took another slow, deep breath, then straightened, wincing in the process. "I think I was just so busy trying to keep up that I didn't realize what a toll the run was taking."

A frown tugged at her brow and hurt knifed through her. "It's my fault. I shouldn't have pushed so hard knowing you were trying to keep up." She gulped in another ragged breath. "I'm sorry. Let's walk from here to cool down our muscles."

He nodded, managed a crooked smile. "That'd be helpful."

The journey back to the house was made in silence. On the one hand Caroline kept beating herself up for not considering his condition. On the other she kept telling herself that she couldn't trust this new, needy Justin. She just wasn't sure she could survive allowing herself to believe, allowing a true physical relationship only to learn later that it had been a mistake. A neuron activity blip related to the trauma of the crash that would never reoccur.

She had to protect herself.

On the long, shaded porch that stretched across the back of the house, Justin hesitated. "Thanks for being so understanding. I know this is difficult." He stared down at the floor for a time. "Coming back after three months...well..." His gaze met hers. "I know it has to be hard. The last thing I want is to make it harder than it has to be."

She couldn't help herself. She had to touch him. Moving in close enough to lay her hand on his chest, to feel his heart beating beneath her palm, she looked directly into those worried blue eyes.

"Everything is going to be fine, Justin. Please don't worry about...*us*...we're fine."

That piercing gaze turned more uncertain...more questioning. "Then why do you tense each time I touch you? Why haven't you even kissed me? Was I that much of a monster before? Did I do something terrible to hurt you? I swear I don't remember. I..."

His words trailed off as the cloud of anguish descended fully on that handsome face. "I swear I'll make it up to you."

Her heart stumbled at his heartfelt words. How did she answer a question like that? This was everything she'd ever wanted...the very words she'd prayed he would say to her. But could she trust this new Justin...this stranger?

"Justin, I—"

"Shhh." He pressed a finger to her lips. "Let's not talk," he murmured.

And then he kissed her.

So softly...so tenderly. Yet the sensation of his firm, masculine lips on hers burst inside her with all the force of a nuclear blast. White-hot heat flashed through her as the fallout rocked her very soul.

She flattened her other palm on his chest, pushed her

hands up and over that sculpted terrain to tangle in the long hair at his nape. Her body molded to his, feeling the heat and power of male muscle. His tongue thrust into her mouth and she moaned with the pleasure of his possession. He tasted hot and wild…and hungry.

He wanted her.

She wanted him.

Did anything else matter?

She stilled, drew her mouth away from the heat and promise of his. Her gaze locked fully with his and in that instant she knew the truth.

Everything mattered.

She'd made that choice a long time ago. Renewed it six months ago when she assumed the office of president. She had to take this slowly…had to be certain.

He smiled. "We have plenty of time," he murmured as if he'd read her mind yet again. "I won't let you down."

How could he have known that those were exactly the words she'd needed to hear?

Chapter Five

"Sir?"

Director Richard O'Riley looked up from the report he'd started to review and found Dupree hovering in the doorway to his office. His secretary hadn't warned him. Center's senior intelligence analyst had most likely asked her not to—which meant only one thing: O'Riley wasn't going to like this.

He motioned for the younger man to step inside. As he did, Dupree closed the door. Another bad sign.

He stationed himself front and center before O'Riley's desk and didn't bother to sit down.

"Sir." He swallowed visibly. "Marsh's body has been found."

If he'd said "Your ex-wife is on the phone begging for a reconciliation," O'Riley wouldn't have been more surprised. He'd expected Marsh to be found—*alive*.

He'd needed him alive. That he was dead complicated O'Riley's life considerably.

"Where?" The hollow word echoed in the seconds of silence that followed.

Dupree cleared his throat. "At the Lincoln Memorial, sir. There…there was a dead…ah…stuffed…ah…"

"For God's sake, Dupree, spit it out!" O'Riley barked coming to his feet. Hell, how could what he had to say next be any worse than what he'd said so far? Marsh was dead. Leaving them no place to go and with nothing new to go on even if they had a direction.

"He had a dead pigeon stuffed in his mouth."

Defeat sucked O'Riley back down into his chair. A warning. "I don't want the media to get wind of this."

"No, sir. D.C.'s Metro kept the part…about the pigeon quiet. The homicide detective feared they might have a new kind of psycho serial killer on their hands."

O'Riley nodded. "Good. I want his body back here ASAP. Get Fitzgerald on this. If we can retrieve any recent memories we need them."

"He's preparing for departure as we speak."

Surprised, O'Riley peered up at the young man who more often than not got on his last nerve, but who was the very best they had. "Good work, Dupree."

Dupree pushed into place what he no doubt considered a smile, but the expression looked more like a facial twitch. "Thank you, sir."

O'Riley considered the other necessary steps, then asked, "Anything found with the body? ID? Papers?"

"Only his wallet, which was empty. No driver's license, no credit cards, no cash. Nothing. They ran his prints which alerted us to the situation."

"Go with Fitzgerald. I want you to ensure that nothing gets lost in the transport. Review the photos from the scene, interview the officers involved and any witnesses who may have stumbled over the body. Someone had to report it. Make sure anyone who came near that body left it the way they found it."

Dupree nodded, a real smile beaming from his face this time. "Will do, sir."

As the intelligence analyst hurried to do his director's bidding, O'Riley let go a heavy exhale. Damn, he'd needed Marsh alive. If Fitzgerald couldn't retrieve some sort of clue as to where he'd been all this tme and who he'd associated with, they were screwed. He would be forced to wait for the other side to act, leaving him with no other option except to react, always the worst-case scenario.

Heaving another disgusted breath, O'Riley put through a call to Winslow's secure line. There was no point in putting off the inevitable. He would learn Marsh's fate within hours and then he'd be pissed that O'Riley hadn't kept him informed. Only a select few were aware of Marsh's connection to Center. But even those few could cause trouble.

Center represented the kind of project that won and lost elections for politicians leading all the way up to the president him- or herself. Winslow wouldn't be immune, nor would anyone else who served as a member of the Collective. No one could know their secrets. Marsh had known almost everything. If he'd passed that information on to the wrong people the result could be calamitous for the entire nation. The encryption codes the military used had been created by Center. There wasn't a scientist or analyst, much less a cryptologist at NSA who could hold a candle to the caliber of personnel on Center's staff.

Any kind of leak could cause a major setback. One on the level Marsh represented would be devastating.

That kind of publicity coupled with the faction working against the president could destroy Center altogether. One way or another they had to discover what Marsh had been up to and with whom. Equally important, they had to protect the president. If her enemies gained power, the fight would be lost. O'Riley feared that Vice President Redmond may have sold out to the same group the former president had gone into collusion with. Whatever else happened, they had to keep that bastard out of the Oval Office.

The Collective wouldn't give the word to take him out without indisputable evidence of his guilt. That wouldn't be easy. O'Riley laughed, a self-deprecating sound. How the hell could they possess the most highly skilled technicians and analysts on the planet and still not be able to solve a mystery so simple?

Someone had killed Daniel Archer, the scientist who'd helped make the Enforcers a success, in an attempt to steal his secrets. Center had been successful in uncovering part of the traitorous scheme. Former UN Secretary General Donald Thurlo had been taken out of the picture. One of Daniel Archer's closest family friends had also been revealed as a traitor. He had admitted that he'd been working with Joseph Marsh in an attempt to steal Archer's files on his super-gene research better known as the Eugenics Project. Now Marsh was dead. Their investigation had hit a brick wall. How could Center possess such power, such genius and not be able to solve a puzzle so seemingly simple?

Winslow would ask that same question.

Too bad O'Riley didn't have an answer for him.

Safe House
48 Hours Remaining

AFTER THE morning briefing Caroline reviewed and signed the necessary documents her secretary had had couriered over by Rupert. She tucked the documents into the pouch and looked up at her senior advisor.

Happiness stretched across her lips for the first time in a long time. Justin didn't remember the awful ultimatum she'd given him and he appeared desperate to make things right. She wasn't ready to trust that possibility just yet, but she wasn't going to rule it out completely either. She wanted a real marriage…children. Her life with Justin would be the quickest solution to the problem. And it wasn't as if she didn't care for her husband. She was certainly attracted to him on a whole new level now. Perhaps absence really did make the heart grow fonder.

"Rupert, I'm really pleased with the progress your suggestions helped to bring about. The bill zipped through with hardly a snag. You were right on all counts."

He nodded an acknowledgment of the compliment. "Thank you, Madam President. I can't take full credit, however. A little bird told me how desperate they were to get that particular budget passed. The anti-smoking reform was scarcely noticed. If all goes as planned, health-care providers will be required to provide more aggressive coverage for kicking the smoking habit. Burying that kind of reform deep in the budget of a more popular, complex bill is always a good strategy."

A very good thing in Caroline's opinion. But there were those who didn't want to pay for smokers' rehabilitation. Stupidly they'd rather pay for the numerous diseases years of smoking wrought while lining their pockets with under-the-table funds from lobbyists supporting the various tobacco and alcohol industries. Any American addicted to drugs of any sort, alcohol and tobacco included, should have the help needed to kick the habit.

"How are things with Justin?" Rupert inquired nonchalantly. "If…I may ask."

Caroline knew there was nothing nonchalant about the question. He was worried about her…still, though she'd slept soundly the past two nights in her husband's arms. Heat seared through her instantly as she remembered that kiss. The way his mouth had claimed hers…the feel of his tongue as he'd explored blatantly. She'd felt his body harden against her. He'd wanted to do more than kiss her…she'd wanted more as well. A shiver swept over her skin. She still wanted more. All of it was so wholly out of character.

"Things are well, Rupert," she said in all honesty. Yes, there were issues that remained, but all in all, things were better.

The look of relief that flooded his expression made her heart glad for such a dear friend. "I'm very glad to hear that, as I am sure your mother will be."

Guilt immediately plagued her. It had been two days and she hadn't even called her mother. Of course, she'd known Rupert would keep her mother informed, but that wasn't the same thing.

"I'll call her today," she said, an apology in her tone. "It's just been so hectic."

"She understands that," Rupert assured her. "How could she have lived all those years with your father and not have understood the frenzy of political life?"

"True," Caroline admitted. Her entire life had been one long, harried roller-coaster ride. But it had been one she wouldn't trade for anything. It was, apparently, in her genes.

"So tell me," she ventured, feeling particularly intrigued, "how is Mother?"

Rupert blushed and shifted in his chair. "You know your mother and I will always be close, Madam President."

Caroline laughed. She hadn't actually expected to get any more than that. "Of course." She gave her old friend a look that said "Drop the Madam President crap."

"But," Rupert ventured, obviously deciding to take her less-than-subtle silent advice, "if more were to come of it, how would you feel about that?"

The unexpected question surprised her...no, it startled her. Was Rupert finally going to make a real play for her mother? Had ten years been long enough for her mother to grieve the loss of her first true love? Yes. Absolutely. More than long enough.

"Immensely relieved," Caroline said bluntly. "It's past time the two of you got on with your lives."

A smile tickled one corner of her old friend's mouth. "I suppose you're right, but I'm not sure your mother sees it that way."

"Give her a push," Caroline suggested. "She won't resist for long." She knew her mother as well as any daughter could. Lora Mattson loved Rupert Downy. She always had, in a way. Her failure to act on that emotion, which had clearly grown over the years, was only due to her undying respect for the husband she'd lost. She hadn't been ready to put the past behind her. Perhaps with a bit of prodding, Rupert could make that happen now. It would please Caroline immensely for her mother to be happily married again.

Perhaps she was finally going to have the opportunity herself. *Slow down, Caroline,* she ordered. She had to take this slowly or risk shattering her heart completely.

"Well." Rupert stood. "I should be on my way."

Caroline rose and handed him the pouch. "Be safe."

"You needn't worry. Levitt and Copeland are making sure of that. They won't let anyone close to this place. My driver had to rendezvous with their security detail about twenty-five miles from here. Then the diversionary route took a full hour. If I understood Copeland right, they have dozens of variations of those routes. No one gets brought in or out the same way twice."

Copeland and Levitt were thorough. The best of the

best. If anyone could protect her, they could. "Enjoy your drive back to civilization then."

She skirted her desk and gave Rupert a quick hug. That was one good thing about working from a remote location, she didn't have to stand so carefully on formality.

"Give my best to Justin," he offered as they strode to the door of her office.

"I'll do that." Caroline wondered as she watched Rupert go where Justin had been this morning. His side of the bed had been cold when she'd awakened. After coffee and a Danish she'd closed herself up in her office for the usual briefings and then Rupert had arrived. She glanced at the clock, 11:00 a.m. What had he been doing with himself all this time?

She closed the door and walked slowly back to her desk. Perhaps he'd had business to attend to as well. A smaller office, complete with everything he would need was housed on this floor as well. Justin had likely taken possession of that one.

It hadn't crossed her mind to ask him if he planned to step back into his role as partner at his computer company or even if he felt up to going back to work. Funny she hadn't thought of that. In fact, she hadn't considered any of the repercussions of his return other than that of their personal relationship. His estate hadn't been probated, since a body had not been found, and she hadn't pursued official proceedings, so that wasn't an issue, but there were other things. She'd had his wardrobe and other personal items stored. She would need to see that they were relocated to their bedroom at the

White House. The small wardrobe that had been supplied for them during their stay here would certainly never be enough. And Justin would want his things returned to their proper place. He'd always been a stickler for organization.

She hadn't actually wanted to store his things, but she'd had no other closure in the matter, so she'd done it. Now it seemed premature. She couldn't change that she'd taken the step, she could, however, reverse that step.

Not wanting to put the task off a moment longer, she made the necessary calls, including one to her mother. As she sat down at her desk her private line rang. She frowned when the caller identification display remained blank. Had Rupert forgotten something? Would his secure cellular number not show up on the unit's readout? Since they had arrived, the only time that line had rung was for the morning briefings or whenever Rupert called. Had his number shown up before? She hadn't noticed.

Gingerly she reached for the receiver, then chastised herself for behaving so foolishly. It wasn't going to bite her. "Hello," she said expectantly.

"Caroline…"

Fear slammed into her chest. Why would Justin be calling her? He was…here… He wouldn't need to call.

"Justin?"

"Help me…"

The voice trailed off with those two anguished words. "Justin!"

A succession of clicks then the dial tone echoed in

her ear. She stared at the receiver, her heart thudding painfully. Had someone kidnapped him…was he lost on the vast property?

She didn't wait for her brain to analyze and evaluate the possibilities. "Agent Copeland!" she shouted as she raced toward the door. He would be right outside. Never more than a few feet away.

"Agent—"

The door burst open two seconds before she reached it. "Madam President?" Copeland filled the doorway, his weapon palmed, his gaze immediately taking in the room around her.

"Where's Justin?" she asked, fighting the hysteria climbing into her throat. She'd only just gotten him back. Things were…different…better. She didn't want to lose him again. They finally had a chance. The memory of that kiss…of the way he'd made her feel made her want to weep.

Two more agents joined their superior, weapons drawn.

"Get me a twenty on Mr. Winters," Copeland said into his communication piece located on his lapel.

Caroline didn't hear the response since it would go directly into his earpiece but she watched the changing expressions on his face. The blood roared so loudly in her ears she felt lightheaded with the sound of it, the feel of it coursing through her veins.

Please, let him be safe…

Footsteps sounded in the entry hall and Justin was suddenly there, his gaze colliding with hers. "What's happened?"

Another agent stood behind him. The one who'd located him, wherever he'd been and given him the news that the president needed him. Not his wife…but the president. No one would ever be so presumptuous as to…

Her mind was rambling. She pushed away the crazy thoughts. "We need some privacy," she said to Copeland. "I'll brief you later."

The agent in charge of her security nodded and cleared the room, closing the door behind him.

Several emotions descended upon Caroline at once with the sound of the door's latch clicking into place.

Only a few days ago it had been speculated that she might be losing her grip on reality because of a call like the one she'd just received. Because of a letter no one had seen but herself and the vice president, who now denied any such knowledge. The caller had been her husband, Justin. She knew his voice. Had known him for more than twenty years. No one could be that good…it had to be his voice.

Until the call had come moments ago, she'd forgotten the horror of hearing his voice on those seemingly nonexistent calls. She'd put the missing letter out of her mind. She'd pushed it all away as if it had not happened because it had been easier to do that than to dwell on the other possibilities.

Her sanity had no longer been in question.

She closed her eyes and drew in a deep bolstering breath. The phone had rung…she had heard the voice. *His* voice.

"What happened?" Justin moved closer, his gaze boring fully into hers as she opened her eyes at the sound of his voice.

For two beats she couldn't bring herself to say the words. She knew already how it sounded. How it would make her look. She did not want to go down that path again…but what choice did she have?

None.

"Where were you?" she asked trying her level best not to sound suspicious or accusing. Dear God, could he really be capable of hurting her this way? It would all make sense. His sudden change of heart. His long absence then his sudden appearance back from the dead. Could he have been in cahoots all along with those who would like to see her out of office? Or was she simply going off the deep end as Redmond suspected? There was only one way to find out.

"I was surveying the grounds. Evaluating security." His expression immediately closed.

Her suspicions rose in tandem with his reaction to her question. Why would he scrutinize her security? He'd certainly never done such a thing before. What did he know about security? She had professionals like Copeland and Levitt who took care of that. Justin knew the caliber of agents who served her. There was no room for doubt.

"Why would you do that, Justin?" She folded her arms over her chest and demanded, "Do you have reason to doubt my security detail's performance?"

Cain took his time before answering her question. Whatever had happened she was shaken. Badly shaken. And it had something to do with him, which was the reason for the underlying annoyance he heard in her tone. He hadn't lied when he'd said he was evaluating her security but he hadn't been that far away. Just outside the house. O'Riley had called him on the secure cellular phone he'd requested from Copeland.

The call had only lasted a couple of minutes. Not that he'd had to worry about a trace or infiltration. Center scrambled all calls. There simply had been no reason to draw out the call. He'd received the latest intel and his instructions had been amended accordingly.

Marsh was dead. He could expect the possibility of change in either timeline or strategy. In other words, his mission status had not changed. He remained on the highest state of alert.

Level VII.

To his knowledge Center had never gone on Level VII before. Even the indiscretion with Archer had only been Level VI, which indicated a serious breach. With a Level VII, however, imminent disaster was presumed.

Cain moved closer to Caroline, using his much larger, physical presence to push her into a reaction. "Your life has been threatened. Isn't that reason enough to distrust anyone and everyone?"

She didn't look away as he'd expected her to do when he paused scarcely two feet from her. He hadn't forgotten that kiss…neither had she, judging by the way her pulse fluttered at the base of her throat and the way her pupils flared. His own body reacted in spite of his tight grip on control. That realization surprised him. He quickly shoved the confusion aside.

"Why are you doing this?" she asked. Her voice quavered ever so slightly.

His gaze narrowed as he attempted to read her. He usually found the task quite easy…effortless almost. But not this time. She'd thrown up a wall between them. Hard as he tried, he couldn't quite penetrate it.

"What is it you think I'm doing?" he asked softly, approaching the matter from a blatantly personal direction.

Her breath hitched as she attempted to fill her lungs. She moistened her lips, then pressed them together for a moment as a new burst of fury flashed in her eyes.

"You made that call. I know it was you. Don't try to pretend it wasn't."

He stared directly into the fire in those lovely eyes. Whatever this was about, she thought he was responsible. "What call?" he countered. She couldn't know about the call from O'Riley. Even if her people had the technology to trace the call he'd received, which they didn't, it was too soon.

"Just tell me the truth, Justin." She lifted her chin and stared back up at him defiantly. "About everything."

Chapter Six

Caroline blinked.

He didn't know.

That was her first impression as she held Justin's gaze two beats longer. His expression was completely open now, allowing her to see that he truly had no idea what she was talking about.

Or was that simply what he wanted her to see?

She wanted to believe him. That realization dawned so swiftly and abruptly that she staggered with the weight of it. She really wanted all of *this* to be real. His kisses…his promises.

She was thirty-seven years old! The president of the greatest nation on the planet. And still she could be reduced to a sap by a man who'd never touched her sexually before that day. A man with whom she'd thought she would spend the rest of her life, share her greatest dreams.

How ironic. No matter what potential one reached, basic human needs never changed. And, by God she would know here and now if he intended to give it to her.

If he were in any way responsible for the calls…the note, the threats to her life. The last sent a cold chill skittering over her flesh. Surely Justin would not wish her harm.

She refused to believe that.

"The truth is," he began, his gaze locked with hers, searching, analyzing, "I only want to protect you. I would never do anything to hurt you."

Cain reached out to her, not with his hands, but with his mind. *I would never do anything to hurt you. Never. I only want to protect you.* She must understand that truth. He needed her complete trust.

She shuddered as his mind touched hers. She wouldn't understand how it happened, would only know that somehow she believed him…or felt his words were sincere. But it would be enough.

"For weeks now," she said slowly as if still uncertain as to whether she should trust him fully, "I've received calls. Only a few, four or five maybe."

"What calls?" He kept his tone soothing, not threatening in any way. Didn't offer to move closer or to touch her. He didn't want to risk breaking the fragile spell his mindwalk had woven. She wanted to believe him…desperately.

"Calls from you." She searched his eyes, looked for any sign of deceit. "While you were in the hospital, is it possible you tried to call me and didn't realize it? Maybe even while still in some form of coma?"

This was something Center hadn't been informed of. Cain wondered who she had shared this information with. "I don't think so." He shrugged for good measure.

"I'm not sure there was even a phone in the room. Who's investigating the calls?"

She moistened her lips again. His gaze followed the motion of her pink tongue and his mouth parched. He blinked, confused once more by the sensations looking at her generated in him. He felt a tightening that made him want to touch her.

"There's nothing to investigate." She said the words with strength and conviction, but her eyes, her expression belied her tone. Vulnerability shimmered in her eyes, trembled on her lips. "No unexplained calls showed up on the register of incoming calls or on the main system voice mail. I even added an answering machine to my private line just for my own peace of mind after that but I haven't received another call. Not until today, but there's no answering machine here and there was no number on the caller ID unit. And…the letter disappeared."

A frown worked its way across his brow. "What letter?" Something else Center hadn't heard about.

"It was faxed directly to the machine in my office." Caroline wasn't making sense, she knew she had to get a firmer hold on her emotions. She looked away in an attempt to hide the weakness she did not want him to see in her eyes. She'd read the letter over and over…had shared it with Redmond. But he'd later insisted that he had seen no such letter. He'd admitted to her having told him that she received one but nothing more.

"It was your handwriting," she told her husband, then shook her head, confusion churning inside her. She had received the letter. It had been his handwriting. She hadn't imagined it. "You needed my help." Her gaze collided with his once more. "Just like in the calls."

"A handwriting analyst confirmed your suspicion?" He watched her closely now as if he expected her to fall apart at any second.

The idea that her vulnerability showed so clearly infuriated her all the more. She was stronger than this. What was wrong with her? Maybe she was losing her grip on reality.

"No," she said sharply, too sharply. She regretted the outburst immediately. Just another indicator of how very close she was to the edge. "The letter disappeared before I could have anyone take a look at it."

"Did anyone else besides you see it?" he asked.

The question was completely logical. She knew it was but it made her want to scream all the same. "Yes!" She stared into those assessing eyes and said the rest. "But he has no recall of the incident so I guess the real answer is no."

"Who?"

She closed her eyes and drew in a breath to bolster her wavering courage. "Redmond," she admitted. "I showed it to him, but he swears I didn't."

"What about the monitors?"

She'd thought of that as well. Certain White House offices were monitored 24/7, had been in one way or another since before the Nixon administration. It preserved a certain level of honesty and integrity within those walls. "I met him for lunch to discuss the matter. I needed privacy, now I wish I hadn't."

"What about when you received the fax? That should have been documented as well."

She laughed, the sound bitter even to her own ears. "Of course it was, but the fax I read wasn't the one they found on my desk with the time and date stamp that matched the one on the video recording of my actions when it was played back."

Justin nodded. "The tape could have been altered."

She had to turn away from him. Emotion surged into her eyes, burning, threatening her hold on composure. She had so wanted to hear those words. To have him believe her above all else. But it sounded unreasonable even to her. Who would have access to the monitoring system? Someone on her staff. She had handpicked most of her staff. What did that say about her judgment? She remembered well how even Copeland had looked at her when she suggested that very thing. He'd thought she was out of her mind. Of course he would never have said so and was only too happy to call in the FBI and start an official investigation if need be. But the risk of anyone finding what could be the truth had been too great.

Caroline Winters might just be losing her mind.

She wouldn't take the risk. Rupert had worried about her. Had almost talked her into relinquishing her post for a time. Maybe she should have.

"Thank you for having so much faith in me, Justin." She met his gaze once more. At least he appeared to believe her. "I didn't pursue the matter. But now…"

Her words trailed off but he knew the rest. She'd

gotten another call and now she wondered. Was she losing it or was someone playing a very dirty game? Maybe even him.

"Caroline." He took her hands in his. "You have to believe me when I say I would never be involved with anything that would hurt you." Cain had grown so accustomed to using Justin's tone and cadence that he did it now without thought. He knew that was important to the mission, but on some level he suddenly felt as if he'd lost something of himself. Another peculiar feeling. "Please let me handle this. I know people who might be able to help."

She shook her head, bewildered. "What people? I have the best—"

"Just let me look into it," he urged. "Let's not bring anyone on your staff into this until we have to. We need to be sure who we can trust."

She didn't answer right away, simply stared into his eyes, assessing. "All right. We'll do this your way for a little while."

Cain considered that step a major milestone in gaining her full confidence. The need for her complete trust might not become an issue but if it did, he felt reasonably sure that he was halfway there.

DIVERSIONARY ROUTE SIX took twice as long to reach civilization as the route they'd taken when she came to the safe house some forty-odd hours ago. Maybe more. But who was counting?

Caroline stared out at the passing landscape in an effort to ignore the mounting tension inside the car. Both Copeland and Levitt had insisted on accompanying her. Justin sat silently at her side. All were immensely annoyed that she would not be swayed from her decision.

After the call and then her blunt discussion with Justin she'd needed to talk to someone neutral. Someone who didn't care about position and power or anything else related to the White House. Dennis Patrick was her friend. They'd attended Harvard together. She'd walked away a civil attorney, he a psychiatrist. The only difference was he made a great deal more money than she did. The idea brought a smile to her lips. He loved bragging about that fact, had teased that the pressure of her "job" was not in keeping with the salary

That was what she loved most about Dennis. He didn't take himself or anyone else too seriously. Right now she needed that kind of objectivity.

Yes, leaving the compound was a risk. But she would not be held prisoner. Precautions yes, but nothing more. This weekend was more about coming to terms with Justin's return than with keeping her safe. At least that's what she'd told herself repeatedly since agreeing to come here.

She'd called Dennis and insisted that they have lunch to discuss recent developments privately. Her phones were monitored. Her every move was watched. If she thought about it for too long it could make her seriously uneasy.

But she didn't. It was the fact of her life at this time and, if she were really lucky, would be for another term after this one.

When they arrived at the small town some twenty miles away—that actually took thirty-five miles to reach from the safe house—Copeland received a call from the advance security team, which was already in place and had already scoped out the restaurant as well as the town. Arrangements had been made for her lunch to be served in a room reserved for parties. Security had told the restaurant owner that she was a diplomatic VIP visiting from Germany. The owner had assured complete privacy from employees as well as customers.

True to his word the rear parking lot had been cleared except for one car, a luxury BMW that belonged to Dennis. A six-man security team waited to escort her into the room through the rear of the restaurant, including the kitchen which had temporarily been cleared for her walk-through. Justin had refused to stay behind at the safe house, but now remained with Copeland since she had not invited him to join her. She needed this time alone with her friend. Levitt stationed himself just inside the room where she and Dennis would dine. The small party room seated about twenty in Caroline's estimation. Dennis waited there with a big grin on his face.

"Wow," he exclaimed facetiously. "When you make an entrance, you really make one, don't you?" He stood as she approached him, then bent to brush a kiss on her cheek. "Good to see you, Caroline."

She hugged him, couldn't resist the temptation. Dennis had always been such a special friend. One who completely understood her psyche. But then, that was his job, wasn't it? But this wasn't about work, this was about being friends in the purest sense of the word.

He pulled out her chair, then took his own. "So, tell me what's going on with you. I saw the press conference." He threw up his hands in amazement. "It's astounding that Justin was in a coma in that hospital all that time."

She nodded, then sipped her water which had already been tested for drugs or other toxins, as her food would be. "It's incredible that no one who worked there ever realized who he was. But from what they told me he looked a mess when he arrived. His hair and beard were overlong. His injuries were their primary concern. They felt certain he would die." Her eyebrows pushed upward in punctuation of her next statement. "Not to mention that they had him pegged as some fugitive from justice."

Dennis laughed. "Oh, I'm sure that sat well with Justin when he woke up."

Caroline frowned as she considered their initial reunion as well as the time since then. "He hasn't complained actually." How could she have forgotten after five years of marriage what a stickler for details Justin was? He'd always gotten annoyed when things didn't go as planned. He'd never allowed the minor schedule changes or missing buttons on a suit returned from the cleaners just to roll off his back. He'd fussed and fretted until he had set things to right whenever possible. Just another of the changes in his personality since waking from that coma. She hadn't thought of that until this second.

"That's a good thing," Dennis assured.

Salads were served by one of the agents on her security detail. Levitt and Copeland didn't want any up-close-and-personal interaction between her and the restaurant's staff.

"I suppose so," she agreed, distracted by the whole idea. How could she have locked away so much in those three months? It was as if she'd purposely forgotten all the unpleasant things about her marriage.

"Tell me what's up. You sounded a little upset when you called." Dennis dug into his salad as if he were ravenous. It was past two, she imagined he normally had lunch before now. How had he assessed her emotional state so easily? Well, that's why they paid him the big bucks, she mused.

"Remember those calls I told you about?" Dennis was the only human being on the planet she'd told other than Redmond, Copeland, and Rupert and those three had been necessary.

Dennis nodded as he chewed.

Caroline picked at her own salad and considered how to tell him the rest. "Well, they couldn't find the calls on the incoming call log. And then there was the letter that was faxed to me."

"What letter?" His gaze narrowed. "Have you been holding out on me, Caroline?" he asked jokingly but there was a kind of seriousness beneath the tease.

She shrugged. "It was his handwriting. I know it was."

"The content please," Dennis urged.

"'Caroline, help me,'" she recited the three words on the handwritten note.

"You're certain this was his handwriting? It could have been from someone who wanted you to believe it was Justin's. Just like the calls. Some forgeries are almost impossible to tell from the real thing."

She sighed. "I know. Rupert insists that's the case." She rolled her eyes. "Now Redmond, well he believes I imagined all of it."

"He's an ass," Dennis said flatly. "I don't like him. Never have." He pointed at her with his fork. "If you remember correctly I told you as much at that first dinner you invited me to before you announced him as your running mate."

If he only knew how right he was. "Perhaps you're right."

Something changed in his expression. "Has something more than what you've told me happened? Something involving Redmond?" He said the last with a scowl. During her hesitation he added, "I hate that bastard."

She was beginning to feel the same way. "He's been working on my staff, undermining loyalties. Tossing out innuendoes to the Cabinet, leaking the crap you read to the press."

"You're kidding!" Dennis's astonished look combined with his disdainful exclamation made her laugh.

Caroline just couldn't help it. Maybe it was hysteria, whatever it was, she laughed long and hard before abruptly pulling herself back together. "Unfortunately it's true. He's been so successful even Rupert suggested I invoke the Twenty-Fifth."

Dennis's eyes were the ones rolling this time. "Oh,

my God! This just gets better and better. I hope you told him to kiss your—"

"I almost took his advice," she said before he could finish the crude statement. Dennis might be a polished Harvard graduate, but he called 'em like he saw 'em.

"Thank God your good sense overrode his temporary insanity."

She let go another sigh. "I wish I could claim that foresight. Actually the call that Justin had been found stalled the action. But Redmond knows how close I was and is still pushing for me to take some time, as he puts it." She forced a pained smile.

"How thoughtful of him," Dennis deduced. "Forget about those senior White House *officials* for now and tell me about Justin."

While they finished their salads and moved on to the main course of pork roast and steamed vegetables, Caroline told him all that had unfolded in the past three days. He stopped her occasionally for clarification but otherwise remained silent, except for the clink of silver against china, as she talked.

"What do you think?" she asked when she'd finished her lengthy monologue and had given him a couple of minutes to absorb all that she'd related.

He swallowed then cleared his throat. Looking thoughtful, he offered, "It's not uncommon for survivors of catastrophic tragedy to do a complete turnaround." He shrugged. "Hell, it's not unusual for those who awaken from prolonged coma to have a new zest for life. He could be genuinely interested in a new start."

That was, in a nutshell, exactly what she'd wanted to hear and yet the hesitation was still there. "But how can I be sure it'll last?"

Dennis made a skeptical sound that wasn't quite a laugh. "You want assurances? Get real, Caroline."

For the first time since they'd sat down Copeland shot Dennis a look. Caroline arrowed Copeland an assuring look. Dennis was her friend. He could be loud, yes, but he meant no disrespect. She knew he wouldn't dream of speaking to her in that manner in public.

"I've been through three marriages and countless relationships," he added, his tone a little subtler. "There are no assurances."

"That may be," she said pointedly, suddenly wondering why she would ask a thrice-divorced man for marital advice, "My feelings aren't the only ones involved here. I want some assurances that I'm not about to plunge headlong into a huge mistake."

"Well, get in line," he said flatly. "Everybody wants to feel confident that a relationship is the right one. That a man or woman with whom they've chosen to move forward into marriage or similar commitment is the one. It doesn't exist. Do you hear me?" he prodded. "There are no reassurances when you're dealing with other humans. Life is not certain. Nothing is."

He was right. She knew he was. But she didn't have to like it. But taking advantage of Justin if all his faculties weren't in order just didn't feel right. Her uncharacteristic uncertainty on the matter was more about him than about her.

"So what are you saying?" she asked crisply.

"That you go for it," he retorted, "on the condition that you'll still respect me and be my friend in the morning."

Only Dennis could come up with such a self-serving twist on such a hideous cliché.

"Caroline," he said quietly, for her ears only, as he leaned toward her, "go for it. It's perfectly legal. He's your husband, for Pete's sakes. Sleep with the man. Have all the amazing orgasms he can give you. Love it! Get pregnant if your heart so desires. And don't feel even a glimmer of guilt. It's not illegal and it's not a sin. What more could you ask?"

She didn't have to answer. The truth was written all over her face. She saw it in his eyes the moment he looked squarely at her after he'd asked the question.

"You want it all." His head slowly moved from side to side. "Didn't your mother ever tell you that fairy tales don't exist? This is the real world, Caroline. Nothing is ever perfect. You can't have it all, contrary to popular belief, it simply doesn't exist."

"But I want it all," she refuted. "I want love, lifetime commitment, children." She shrugged. "I intend to have the whole fantasy."

He lowered his voice, glanced covertly at their guard and said, "There are drugs for delusions, Caroline. Good drugs. Let me get my 'script pad."

She had to laugh, because she knew from the wicked gleam in his eyes that he was kidding. "You are truly a rotten friend," she tossed back. "I don't know why I keep you." She poked a succulent wedge of roast pork into her mouth and grinned.

"Because I tell you the truth," he said and took another bite himself. "Because I care about you and I would never lie to you. I can't help you with the calls and the letter. My best guess would be that it's someone on the inside with access to tapes of Justin's voice and samples of his handwriting. Whoever is behind these incidents is someone who probably wants you out of the way."

"I agree. I just can't fathom the reasoning. Especially now that Justin is back."

Dennis shrugged. "Who knows? There are some real psychos out there. Keep your people on it." He rested his hand on hers. "As far as your relationship with Justin. Go for it. You both deserve to be happy."

Caroline decided he was right on all counts. She did deserve to be happy. So did Justin. And life didn't carry any guarantees. Waiting on certainties was foolish. One could only go for it and hope for the best.

"You're right, Dennis." She smiled with genuine affection for her old friend. "You always are."

CAIN WALKED directly behind Caroline as she moved back through the restaurant's kitchen headed for the rear exit with her friend, Dennis Patrick, at her side. Copeland and his team were in position around them, a barrier from any and all threat. But Cain's senses had gone on alert.

Something was wrong. He studied Dr. Patrick as he

moved alongside Caroline. The smile, his relaxed posture. The security team looked sharp and ready. Yet, every instinct warned Cain that a move was about to be made.

Outside, the parking lot was still devoid of other vehicles. Only those related to Caroline's arrival and Patrick's occupied the too-quiet setting. Cain surveyed the area, the surrounding rooftops and rear exits of shops and found nothing out of place.

Yet something was.

"We should go," he urged Caroline.

She managed a tight smile, but her eyes were questioning before she turned to her friend. "Thanks for coming, Dennis." She pressed her cheek to his.

"Any time." He gave her a little two-fingered salute. "Keep in touch, Madam President." He looked in Cain's direction. "Good to see you again, Justin. Stay well."

Cain pushed a smile into place and nodded.

He had a feeling that the last had been a mere formality. Ignoring Caroline's husband would not have been proper etiquette.

Patrick turned to go. The hair on the back of Cain's neck stood on end. The flash of something in his peripheral vision jerked his head around.

Without thought or hesitation he shoved Caroline to the ground, absorbing the impact of a bullet a mere fraction of a second after she was out of its path. The inertia of his move combined with the force of the bullet sent him slamming into Patrick. They both tumbled to the ground.

More shots were fired.

Running feet.

Silence.

Chapter Seven

Caroline paced the floor back at the safe house. Copeland had insisted she not accompany Justin to the closest medical clinic. Her husband had insisted as well that his injury was nothing more than a mere flesh wound. Neither man would give an inch and since Justin refused to leave for the clinic until she'd been taken to the safe house, she'd had little choice.

She paused now, halfway across the front room, surveying through the window the long driveway that wound through the trees and toward the highway two miles from her location. She didn't remember her husband being so courageous. Not that Justin had been a coward.

But this had been different. He had spotted the shooter even before her security team. Copeland and Levitt and the others were highly trained bodyguards. Not mere Secret Service agents, but the best of the best, *executive bodyguards*. Perhaps Justin had merely been lucky. Had just happened to look in the right direction at the right moment.

Her gaze narrowed as she replayed the horrific scene in the private theater of her mind. No. His actions had been too precise...too powerful to have been a simple, however fortunate, reaction.

Again the whole scenario of his lying in that hospital bed for three long months didn't sit right with her. What if he'd been somewhere else? Doing something...like training to react as he had today?

Caroline shook her head. There she went with those conspiracy notions again. Dennis would laugh and tell her to get a grip. She closed her eyes and exhaled a heavy breath. Thank God her dear friend hadn't been injured. She and Justin were well aware of the risks they each took, but Dennis had been dragged into this mess because of her. Not that she'd wanted Justin to get hurt. Certainly not.

She threw her hands up and resumed her pacing. Analyzing the situation to death wasn't going to change anything. Her senior advisor and her press secretary had already conference-called her to ensure all was well and to decide on a course of action. That was one annoyance she could do without, but it came with the job. If she broke a nail every one had to be briefed. The press had to be handled.

Okay, so that was an exaggeration, but it was almost that bad. She needed to regain her perspective here. She had just under twenty-four hours before she returned to the District and she needed to make a few decisions— such as how she planned to put Redmond in his place.

Her husband was back now. The caller who wanted to rattle her would eventually be caught or would stop out of boredom when his evil plan didn't garner the desired reaction. She would spend the next few hours setting her affairs with Justin to rights. She wasn't completely sure what all that would entail. Though to some degree she fully agreed with Dennis's conclusion, a part of her just wouldn't allow her to dive in too quickly. It was that conservative side she'd inherited from her mother. Her father had warned her that it would be the bane of her existence at times and he'd been right.

She fully intended to get her personal agenda in order and then proceed onto matters at the White House. Enough was enough, and she'd had enough.

A surge of adrenaline poured through Caroline and she felt stronger than she had in a very long time. Terrorists weren't going to keep her from doing her job. And whoever had been taunting her were nothing more than terrorists.

The people were counting on her.

Finally the big black SUV came into view as it emerged from the treed canopy of the long drive. Caroline's heart rushed into her throat. They were back!

She moved to the entry hall but Levitt halted her with an uplifted hand. "Stand by, ma'am," he said firmly. They're coming right in. I'd rather you stay inside."

Though she hated the idea of cowing to the threat, she knew Agent Levitt was right. Going outside would not only risk her life but Justin's and the accompanying security members.

The door finally opened and Justin walked inside,

followed by Copeland and three of his men. Her husband's jacket was missing and the left sleeve of his shirt had been cut away. A white gauze bandage covered a portion of his upper arm. An ache pierced her at the memory of his pushing her out of the way and taking that bullet intended for her.

Maybe he really did love her in the way she longed for him to. The accident had apparently changed him. Perhaps the words that inspired such longing in her weren't just talk.

"Are you all right?" She went to him, touched his injured arm. "How bad is it?"

He patted her hand soothingly. "Just a flesh wound. It'll heal in no time."

"Thank you, Agents Copeland and Levitt," Caroline said. "We'll be in our suite."

The two agents nodded their understanding and Caroline walked arm-in-arm with Justin to the staircase.

"Did the doctor give you something for pain?"

"That wasn't necessary," he assured her as they climbed the stairs. "It's really not that bad."

Once they'd reached their room and the door was closed, blocking out all else, Caroline turned to him. "Justin, you scared me to death." She blinked at the emotion welling in her eyes. "I thought I was going to lose you again."

Cain sensed that she needed to be held, comforted. He took her into his arms and said the words she needed to hear. "I'm fine. Everything is fine. You don't need to worry anymore."

He held her that way for a very long time, and then she drew back and led him to the bed. It wasn't a gesture designed to seduce him, but an expression of her need to stay close while she rested. He could feel her exhaustion. She was so very tired. So he crawled onto the bed with her and held her while she slept.

Hours later he slipped away, leaving Caroline sleeping peacefully. He doubted she'd had much sleep in several days, maybe even weeks. The calls and letter she'd told him about today were things Center needed to know about. The attempt on her life they would have heard about already. Considering this newest turn of events, he needed to ensure his orders had not changed.

Cain eased from the room and went in search of a private place where he could make his call. It was dark outside. The dark had always been his ally.

He made his way to the kitchen where a member of security stopped him at the rear door. "Good evening, Mr. Winters."

"I'm taking a walk." His tone left no room for argument. Neither did the intense gaze he leveled on the younger, smaller man. The gun tucked into the shoulder holster beneath that suit jacket would not begin to even the odds.

"Would you like someone to accompany you, sir?"

"No thanks."

The agent opened the door for him. "Don't wander far from the house, sir."

"Got it."

Cain stepped out into the night air, noting the distant

smell of rain. Considering the cloud cover a storm appeared to be brewing. Depending on what O'Riley had to say there might be more than one storm headed his way.

He entered the number for O'Riley's secure line and waited. Cain didn't have to wonder if the director would be there. He never left Center when a Level V or higher mission was ongoing. He answered on the first ring.

"O'Riley," he growled, his voice gravelly from too much coffee, too little sleep or maybe both.

"Cain reporting in."

"What the hell happened this afternoon?"

Cain quickly retold the events that had taken place at the restaurant.

"And no one but the security team and the shrink knew about the plans to meet?"

"Only the security team. Dr. Patrick didn't know the actual location until he arrived there."

O'Riley remained silent for a moment but he didn't have to say anything, Cain knew exactly what he was thinking. This looked more and more like an inside job of an even closer nature than they'd first concluded. And someone wasn't doing a very good job of keeping it under wraps. The whole scenario was almost too obvious.

"How badly were you wounded?" his superior wanted to know.

"Just nicked the skin and muscle of my left forearm, nothing serious." The pain was all but gone now.

"You'll have to keep the bandage on even after it heals or she'll notice."

Cain was well aware of that fact. Since he was a

speed healer there would scarcely be any indication of the wound by the day after tomorrow. He would need to ensure that she didn't see the area where it had been.

"Make sure she isn't out of your sight from now on," O'Riley ordered. "I don't like that they took her back to the safe house while you were taken in the other direction for medical care."

Cain's gaze came to rest on the window to the room where she slept. "I didn't like it either, but refusing to go would have been out of character. Insisting that her safety be risked further by dragging her along would have been as well. She is already watching me closely. I couldn't risk blowing my cover entirely."

Another long pause.

Cain waited, his respiration and heart rate remaining exactly the same. O'Riley considered his lengthy moments of silence to be intimidating, but nothing intimidated Cain. O'Riley, of all people, should know that by now.

"Do you have additional orders?" Cain asked, refusing to waste his time on games.

"No," his director admitted. "Just keep her safe. This incident had nothing to do with our diversionary tactics."

Center had, at first, leaked the possibility of a threat that had the presidential security personnel jumping through hoops. Center had wanted increased security around her and with Redmond's continued interference the only way to ensure that step was to instigate a bogus assassination threat—the mechanical failure on Air

Force One. But now the threat had morphed into reality, not emanating from Center, of course.

"Is there anything else I should know?" O'Riley prodded as Cain remained silent.

"A few weeks ago she started to get calls," he said slowly, considering his words carefully so as not to give away her proximity to the edge where those calls were concerned. Cain didn't understand his sudden need to protect her in this way. It wasn't rational or logical. It simply was.

"There was a letter faxed to her as well but it disappeared. All of the same approximate content—her husband pleading for help. Whenever the calls were looked into, nothing was found."

"And no one believes that she really received the calls or the letter," O'Riley guessed.

"It looks that way."

"We'll patch into the lines at the White House, see what we can find. She received a call at her current location as well?"

"Today."

"I'll let you know when Dupree has anything to report."

"She insists on returning to the White House tomorrow morning. If Redmond makes a move—"

"You'll stop him."

"Understood."

Cain disconnected and tucked his phone back into his pocket. He inhaled deeply of the night air, listened to the night sounds and watched the window where she slept.

If the vice president made an overt move Cain was

to take him out. Survival would be highly unlikely. But then, all Enforcers knew that they were expendable. No Enforcer was more important than the mission.

The mission was all that mattered.

Cain returned to the house, nodded to the agent still posted at the rear entrance. Others would have been walking the grounds but Cain would have known if one had come within hearing distance of him. His night vision as well as his hearing was superior.

Hesitating before going back upstairs, Cain decided he needed to eat. He imagined Caroline did as well. Thinking of her in that way would only add to his appeal. That he considered her needs without forethought gave him pause…but that was his mission. Wasn't it?

He prepared a tray with various cheeses, crackers, fruit and wine. The kitchen was well stocked and offered every imaginable amenity. He placed two stemmed glasses and linen napkins on the tray and said goodnight to the agent as he left the room.

Upstairs, the room was still dark which meant Caroline had not awakened yet. She obviously needed the rest. Cain suspected that she pushed herself entirely too hard. But that went with the territory he supposed, and she would not possess the superior stamina he did. He wondered at that…marveled at the idea that she would carry on despite her weariness. For him, determination and single-minded intensity were encoded in his genetic makeup. He wondered what drove her. Shaking his head, he forced the idea away.

It made no difference.

He set the tray on the table near the broad expanse of windows and turned on a nearby floor lamp. A soft glow illuminated the far side of the room so as not to intrude too much on the moonlight now shining through the windows. Surprisingly, the storm he'd anticipated had passed them by, unveiling the moon. He wondered if Caroline Winters would be so lucky with the other storm. He doubted that possibility.

"Justin?" The sound of her soft voice pulled his attention toward the bed. She lay there, her white dress rumpled and in stark contrast to the royal-blue comforter draping the bed.

"I thought you might be hungry." He gestured to the tray and offered the expected smile.

She eased up to a sitting position. "You shouldn't have done that. I could have scrounged up something." She looked from his face to his left arm and he knew she was wondering about his arm.

"I'm fine." He bent his arm and straightened it to prove his words. "It barely hurts."

She pushed her long dark hair from her face as she scooted off the bed and he found himself captivated by the way the silky strands fell over her shoulder. He had the inexplicable urge to touch her hair. Illogical, he knew. She walked toward him, her long legs covering the distance in only a few steps. She had a well-proportioned body and looked strong for one so slender. He liked that very much. Liked looking at her.

Watching her was his mission.

All the better if he found his work pleasant.

"Yummy," she murmured as she reached for a couple of grapes and popped them into her mouth. "Hmmm."

Remembering the other necessary steps, he poured the wine he had already uncorked. The sound of it sloshing into the glasses filled the quiet of the room as she watched him. Abruptly he wondered if she found watching him a pleasant experience.

She took the glass he offered, sipped the wine and moaned her pleasure. "Excellent." Reaching for a serving of peppered cheese she asked, "Did you mean the things you said to me earlier today?" She chewed thoughtfully for a moment. "About wanting to make things right between us."

"Of course. I meant every word. Why do you doubt me so?"

The question surprised Caroline. He should know better than anyone, but then he might see the past differently than she did, or maybe he truly didn't remember.

She set her glass aside and splayed her hands. "Justin, maybe you don't remember, but things had been…" She searched for the right word. "Things had been strained for quite some time. We…" Despite the fact that he was her husband—that he had at one time known the truth—she found saying the reality of their marriage out loud more than difficult. "You told me you weren't interested in a physical relationship with me. You tried…I think." She frowned, peered up at him, hoping to save herself further humiliation. "Don't you remember? How can you expect me just to believe that everything will be just as it should be from now on?"

This time he did hesitate but not for long. "I was a fool. I have no other explanation." He set his glass aside and took her hands in his. "I admit that I can't remember everything about our life together, but I do know that I intend it to be different now."

She wanted so to believe that. Wanted to hold on to the promise with both hands. Dennis had told her to go for it. Why couldn't she just do that? It would be so simple. But she wasn't sure her heart could take the hurt if Justin changed his mind later on or reverted to his old ways. She might be strong, but she wasn't that strong.

"I want to believe, Justin," she confessed. "I really do. But the thought of putting my emotions out there on that limb scares the hell out of me."

He took her into his arms and pressed a soft kiss to her forehead. "Then we'll take this slowly. Take our time. See where nature leads us."

Who was this man? Her heart thundered at his words. Justin had never talked this way to her before. Not once. "All right. Slow, easy. We'll see where it leads."

"But now we eat." He pulled out her chair and settled her at the table. "Eat and enjoy the view." The moon had burst through the clouds and now hung so close it was almost as if she could reach out the window and touch it.

Justin sat down across from her and helped himself to the goodies he'd prepared. Caroline watched, thankful that God had spared his life…had spared hers. That He had given Justin a nudge at just the right moment and ensured their safety. That had to be the answer. To dwell on other possibilities was a waste of time and energy.

Though the shooter had not been caught, they were all alive. That was the most important aspect of the failed assassination attempt.

She refused to consider that the imminent threat had to be coming from one of her own people. Right now she didn't want to think. She wanted to enjoy. She had only a few more hours before returning to the real world. She intended to enjoy every moment of it.

When she'd consumed as much fruit and cheese as she dared and finished off her third glass of wine, Caroline felt reasonably certain she should do the bath thing and go to bed before she lost all control over her tongue and other parts south.

"I'll clean up," Justin said, as if he understood just what she needed when she rose from her chair insisting that she was stuffed.

Her head spinning just a little, she strolled to the en suite bath and sat down on the edge of the tub. As the hot water filled the massive tub she thought of the way he'd rubbed her shoulders their first night here. She giggled when she thought of the possibility of him doing so again tonight. That would be the perfect ending for this day. Something wonderful but not pushing the boundaries just yet. Slowly, he'd promised. They would take it slowly.

She set the whirlpool on low. Already her muscles ached to feel the swirling heat. Her right hip was a little sore where she'd hit the ground today. When Justin had saved her life, she added to herself with a smile.

Her clothes dropped one garment at a time onto the floor and then she tucked her hair into a knot on top of her head before slipping into the deep water. She groaned with pleasure as she relaxed fully against the backrest.

"Heaven," she murmured.

Another groan echoed her and her eyes snapped open to find Justin watching her from the doorway. She couldn't be sure how long he'd been standing there but from the intense look in his eyes and the rigid stance of his body she'd guess long enough.

She smiled, resisting the urge to issue an invitation for him to join her.

He didn't wait for one. He crossed the room in two long strides and sat down on the edge of the cool marble tub. The sleek, coolness of the marble made the liquid heat all the more enticing.

"Sit forward and I'll rub your back," he suggested softly, his voice rough with desire. The sound sent a tingle straight to her center. She shivered in spite of the heat churning around her.

She didn't answer, just obeyed his request. His hands settled on her shoulders and somehow they felt softer this time, less scarred. The wine, she told herself. She was only imagining that his hands felt softer.

He squeezed and kneaded, rolled and smoothed those strong fingers over her flesh, wrenching moan after moan from her. She clasped her arms around her knees and laid her head there, giving him full access to her back. Those skilled hands trailed down her spine, touching, teasing, making her quiver inside until she could take it no longer.

She straightened and peered up at him, the desire mixed with the lingering effects of the wine making her dizzy all over again. "Thank you," she said softly, when she really wanted to beg him for more. Just as before her insides quivered on the brink of release.

He cupped her cheek and ushered her back against the smooth surface of the tub. "I'm not finished yet," he whispered. A ghost of a smile played about one corner of his mouth as he dropped to his knees next to the tub. One strong hand started to work on her chest, above her breasts. He stroked her shoulders, dipping down to the valley of her cleavage, then upward.

Her eyes closed as she gasped for air. Did he have any idea what he was doing to her? Again and again he soothed that flesh, his fingers never venturing past the rise of her breasts…never dipping into that spot between them that yearned for his touch.

She crossed her legs and tried to slow the throbbing there, but it was no use. The frenzy building would not be denied. She needed more. Wanted more.

Her fingers curled around his wrist and she dragged his hand lower, onto her breast. She whimpered as his fingers closed around it and squeezed. The pulse between her thighs pounded, urging her closer and closer to that place of pure sensations. She arched her back and he used both hands to knead and pump her breasts, squeezing, releasing, and then rolling her rock-hard nipples between his thumbs and forefingers. Again and again he repeated the process, driving her insane. Why didn't he touch her *there*…where she needed to be touched?

His hands never deviated from her breasts, not even skimming her rib cage.

Desperation driving her, she pulled one hand lower, over her rib cage and abdomen, down to the center aching for him. His fingers stilled there, nestled amid the wet curls. She made a sound of need, arched her hips upward in urgency.

"Please," she whimpered, reaching down and pressing his hand harder against that wanton flesh.

He parted her, strummed his thumb over her most sensitive place. She cried out at the sharp stab of desire the move elicited and opened her legs wider in invitation. His fingers moved deeper, sliding easily inside her. The first ripples of orgasm accompanied the move and she cried out again.

He thrust in and out of her, his thumb keeping a steady pressure in just the right spot until she plunged into release. It went on and on and he never let up, kept the rhythm and the pressure on until the final waves receded. Then he lifted her from the tub, water cascading down the front of his body. He set her on her feet and dried every square inch of her, touching and tasting as he went. When his mouth touched her sex, she shook so violently she had to brace against his shoulders to stay vertical.

Sensing her weakness, he carried her to the bed and stripped out of his wet clothes. She gasped at the pure male sight of him…wanted him inside her. To hell with going slowly. But he had other plans. He finished the job he'd started, lathing and sucking her flesh until she exploded into release yet again, and then he covered her with the cool sheet and snuggled up next to her.

His own sex formed a hard ridge against her backside, but he made no move to seek satisfaction. He simply held her until, physically sated and exhausted, she went to sleep and dreamed of how she would spend those final hours of secluded bliss with her husband.

Unspecified Location

"THIS IS twice you've failed."

He laughed at the rebuke. "I think you have me confused with someone else. I had nothing to do with the fiasco in Mexico. That was the other guy."

Ignoring the pointed correction, his displeased employer continued, "In less than twenty-four hours he will be back at the White House. That was not supposed to happen. And yet, because of incompetence it surely will. Our chances of controlling her actions are limited with him there, especially if he talks."

Fury flared, but he tamped it down. He refused to waste the effort. He settled an indifferent gaze on the man who held the other half of his payment ransom and who definitely needed to get his facts straight. "I trust you'll adjust your schedule. The job will be completed. I'm on it now. He's not going to talk."

The heat of anger rushed up the other man's face, turning it bloodred. He smiled, knowing that it did not matter how angry his employer grew, there was nothing he could do. *He* was the only man who could get close enough to get the needed information. And he would ensure the job was done, but he wanted to watch the puppets squirm a bit longer first. His impatient employer didn't have to know that part.

"Every moment Justin is alive is another one in which he might impart what he learned. If that happens—"

"That won't happen." He smiled, loving the confusion on the part of the man who was supposed to be in charge, loving knowing something the boss didn't.

"How can you be certain?" he demanded, his face twisting with the rage he could no longer contain.

"Because he's an impostor."

Shock claimed the crimson face staring at him. "What do you mean? That's impossible. And even if you suspected such a thing, you couldn't be certain."

His smile broadened. "Oh, I'm certain all right. I'm absolutely certain."

His employer stood. "I'm not sure I believe your little theory. Time is wasting. That funding approval has to go through…if it doesn't we all lose. Three days. We have three days before this goes to the next level."

"Maybe you'd better be asking your *other* partner in crime how this happened. I've got a feeling he knows how it came about," he warned. "My source says someone headed off his attempt to separate the two of them in Mexico City. Any idea who would have that kind of foresight? Who knew we were going to strike?"

Judging by the evolving expression on his employer's face, he'd finally made his point.

"Think about it," he went on. "Who has the resources to put a look-alike in place? To head off your plans?

And if it's who I think it is, why didn't your partner warn you?"

The other man's gaze narrowed. "O'Riley." He smiled then. "I should have known."

Chapter Eight

Caroline surveyed the room, the Oval Office, looking from one expectant face to the other. These were her top advisors, the men and women who made up her Cabinet. She'd handpicked each for his or her post. These were the people whom she respected and trusted the most, the ones who were supposed to trust and respect her without reservation. When had the breakdown begun?

"Yes," she confessed in answer to the last question put to her. "I composed the letter." That damned letter still haunted her. She would know who'd faxed a copy to Redmond. At this point she still didn't want to believe it was her personal secretary, but she couldn't rule her out as a suspect just yet. "I thought it would be the right step to take at the time. *If* you read it in its entirety then you know I felt somewhat hesitant about the step. But the security of this country has been and still is my first priority. And, as you well know," she surveyed the group once more, "things have changed. My husband is safe and any other issues related to those three months he was missing have been resolved. I've had a couple of days to relax and I'm ready to get back to work."

"What about the two attempts on your life, Madam President?" Redmond tossed out on the table. "Are you just going to pretend those didn't happen? Wouldn't an extended absence be best for you?"

It would be best for you, she didn't say. "No." She didn't have to scan the faces around the conference table to know that expressions shifted and glances were exchanged. They were all waiting for her to admit defeat…to crumble. How on earth had it come to this?

"I have no intention of turning my back on the duties of my office. I'm perfectly capable of carrying out those duties. Perhaps you have a question about that?" She looked from one face to the next again, allowing the weight of her gaze to press down on each for just the right amount of time. "If there is no question, then I'd like to proceed with business as usual."

She rose from her chair, the act one of dismissal. The others followed suit. Hands reached for hers, each giving a firm shake with the offered parting platitudes. When Secretary of State Samuel Hall took her hand, she held on to his beyond the perfunctory brush of palms. "Can you stay a minute, Samuel?"

He nodded and stepped aside for the others to move past him. When all but Hall and Redmond had exited,

Caroline gifted her vice president with a lackluster smile. "We'll talk later."

"Very well, Madam President." He left, none too happy to be dismissed without additional considerations. Well, too bad. The kid gloves were off now. Caroline didn't trust him and she intended to make no bones about it. She would get this house back in order. She'd had her moment of weakness, of uncertainty. But she was back on track now.

"Madam President," Samuel said when Redmond had left the room, "I've looked into the South American issues as you requested."

A week or so ago, before all the insanity had rocketed so far out of control, she had asked Samuel to head the delegation to look more deeply into the South American situation. He had been focused for so long on the Middle East, as was the Secretary of State before him, that she felt the rest of the world had gone unnoticed. That was a mistake, one this administration might very well live to regret.

"And what is your assessment?" She moved to the comfortable clutch of chairs before her desk and sat down, then gestured to the one adjacent to her. "Please, make yourself comfortable."

Samuel Hall was a tall, broad-shouldered man. His father was African-American, his mother European-American; in Caroline's opinion he possessed the best of all three cultures. The staunch pride and determination of being an American radiated from him. Samuel was one of her strongest supporters. He would never turn his back on her.

She needed him now more than ever.

He sat down and exhaled a heavy breath. "The ever-increasing civil unrest in South America has been overlooked for far too long. I agree with your conclusion in that respect. However, I believe we've had some hand in that."

Her gaze narrowed as she considered that assessment. "In what way?"

"I'm not sure just yet. But I think we have an anti-American faction working behind our backs down there."

She smiled. "Tell me something I don't know, Samuel. Aren't they everywhere?"

He pursed his lips for a moment, considering how he wanted to proceed. "This one is different. This faction appears to be operating in a way far from the typical. I believe our own inner circle of people may be involved."

She looked heavenward and shook her head. Not another conspiracy. "This is truly becoming tedious."

"Madam President." Samuel patted her arm. "Every administration goes through these things. That you're a woman only tosses another aspect into the mix. There are many who want you to fail. Then they could say that the office of president of this country was never meant to be filled by a woman." He patted her arm once more then stood. "But you see, they don't know what I know." He smiled at her.

"And what's that?"

"That you will not fail. That, like your father, you will not give in to the pressure."

When Samuel had left, Caroline considered his parting words. He was right. She would not fail. Her father had been her role model and he certainly never gave up on a fight.

She'd almost, after five years, given up on her husband. That had been a mistake. Her chest suddenly tightened as remembered warmth spread through her. The way Justin had touched her, pleasured her on Saturday night replayed in her mind. She'd waited so long. He'd known and had tried to make it up to her. Then the pleasantness of the day on Sunday. Nothing special. Just quiet time…time shared without animosity or external tension. Only the sweet hum of desire. She'd been fully prepared to make love with him, but he'd merely held her instead, giving her time, allowing her to be sure.

His company had insisted that he take some additional time before returning to the fray of bringing the globe into the ever-evolving world of cyber systems. Justin didn't appear to mind. Though his affiliation was only as an advisor since she became president, the decision surprised her…in a good way. He wanted to stay close to her. He was insisting on accompanying her to the graduation at the Academy of the Holy Cross this evening.

The idea that he wanted to spend as much time with her as possible made her feel complete—invincible. Redmond had better get back in line, for she was not about to be thwarted by him or anyone else. She was back—mind and body. He would see. And anyone who wanted to take his side would fall just as he would if he waited too long to see the error of his ways.

Caroline moved behind her desk and reviewed her

calendar. Remembering the mix-ups and confusion surrounding those last couple of weeks before she took her mini-vacation, she summoned her secretary. If anyone decided to take a potshot at her sanity again, she intended to be prepared.

"Yes, Madam President."

Caroline produced a smile for Barbara. Trust was not the issue, she considered, as her apparently loyal secretary crossed to her desk, it was awareness that Caroline had allowed to falter. She intended to be fully aware of *all* that went on around her henceforth. She would not be caught off guard again.

"Let's go over the calendar."

"Certainly." Barbara took a seat in front of Caroline's desk. "Where would you like to begin?"

"With a new policy," Caroline said bluntly. "From now on, I want you to initial each appointment that you and I have approved. I want the calendar on my desk as well as the one in my PDA to reflect our joint approval."

Barbara nodded once. "Whatever you think is best, Madam President."

Caroline knew exactly what was best for her. She recalled an adage her father had emphasized: complacency was the route to self-ruin. She had a new route now.

A new route and a new attitude.

The Academy of the Holy Cross
Kensington, Maryland

PRIDE FILLING her chest, emotion shining in her eyes, Caroline watched the young women march toward the rest of their lives. The Academy of the Holy Cross had been educating young women since the 1800s. Strength and courage, as well as a strong spiritual conviction, was emphasized. These women now accepting their diplomas represented the cream of the crop and would move on to the finest universities in the country as well as abroad.

Her speech to this class had been meant to inspire these women to the greatness she fully expected each one to achieve. The resounding standing ovation she'd received when she'd finished indicated that she had accomplished her goal. As a graduate of Holy Cross herself, Caroline understood the opportunities that abounded. These women had already been exposed to greatness…understood where they could go if they so choose. Nothing would stop them now. She fully expected to see one of them occupying the Oval Office in the future.

Justin, looking extraordinarily handsome in his dark suit, stood beside her as they applauded the graduating class. Her security detail had faded into the background, appearing to be mere attendees at the festivities. But they were everywhere, watching, waiting for the slightest wrong move. She didn't want any wrong moves tonight. These graduates deserved the perfect night. Every precaution had been taken to ensure Caroline's safety as well as the safety of those in attendance. In fact, she had felt compelled to speak with the principal and warn him that her attendance might not be such a good thing considering all that had happened. He had insisted that she come. The graduating class would be gravely disappointed without her annual appearance.

A small reception had been planned for alumnae members after the ceremony. Caroline looked forward to seeing some of her former classmates. Her gaze lingered on the man at her side. And afterward, anticipation sang through her veins, she wanted to make her and Justin's first night back in the White House special. She needed to begin their second chance on the right foot.

He looked down at her and she couldn't help smiling. He was so very handsome, even with the scar. When he turned back to the cheering crowd her gaze remained fixed on his profile. The scar looked much smaller now. Or was it her imagination? Maybe it had only appeared much worse the first time she saw it. She might simply be adjusting to the changes. She thought of how his hands felt softer now, not so rough. Her gaze moved to those hands, watched as he clapped enthusiastically along with everyone else in attendance. Those scars appeared much less apparent now as well. She dismissed the idea; she had to be mistaken…just her imagination.

That he had declined a complete physical with his personal physician had unsettled her just a little. In the past he'd always done the logical thing. Ensuring that all was as it should be certainly felt like the logical thing to do in Caroline's opinion.

She pushed the troubling thoughts away and focused

on the ongoing festivities. Justin was a very intelligent man. He would do the right thing in his own time.

Tonight, she had to do the right thing…for both of them.

Private Residence
Alumni Reception

CAIN NURSED his drink as he watched the guests mingle and mill about the elegant room. An alumna, a close friend of Caroline's from her school days, had insisted on this exclusive reception for the members of their graduating class who had chosen to attend this year's ceremonies.

The event itself didn't give him pause since it had been planned for two months. Yet the sheer number of guests combined with caterers and hired help made tight security difficult. His instincts were humming tonight and that was not a good sign.

He stayed close to Caroline, despite the fact that four agents mingled among the guests, including Levitt, who didn't veer more than a half-dozen feet from the president's side. Each exterior door as well as each floor of the grand Kensington, Maryland, residence was covered. The gated grounds were being monitored as well. Still, Cain felt on edge. Threat loomed not so far away. He sensed it on every level.

He also sensed difficulty where he and Caroline were concerned. Though he had taken their relationship to a more physical level as he had known would be necessary, he had refrained from taking personal gratification.

Instinct warned him that it would be a mistake, though he could not say how much longer he could put off the inevitable. Caroline Winters was determined.

He understood the human need for physical bonding on an intimate level and she was well overdue. It wasn't that providing the necessary physical union would be unpleasant, it was more about moving beyond some emotional barrier of hers he instinctively understood would be a mistake.

When he touched her he experienced sensations that were completely alien to him. Not unpleasant, he reiterated, merely confusing. He yearned for her even when they were not in the same room. Today, for instance, when she'd been carrying out her presidential duties, he'd had a difficult time thinking of anything but her. Watching her was his mission, but this was different. He wanted to do a great deal more than watch her. He wanted to touch her…to kiss her as he had on the night before last. The sounds she made, the way her body reacted to his touch intrigued him. Made him want to see more. To learn more. That was not part of the mission.

What he felt appeared to be emotion…which was impossible since he possessed none.

When his gaze settled on Caroline once more his entire body reacted, refuting his claim.

The realization startled him…another first.

Unspecified Location

THE DOOR OPENED and his urgent appointment walked in. He watched in utter disdain as the fool took a seat.

He didn't bother standing or even greeting him. This was an unnecessary risk. He already had the intel he was no doubt about to receive. In fact, he wondered if he even needed the fool any longer, considering what he suspected now. But he was a patient man. The idiot might prove useful yet.

"They know it's you," his visitor said, his expression somber, his palms no doubt sweating.

"Of course they do. They have the technology. I assumed that when Marsh's body was discovered they would know the truth within a matter of hours."

Confusion lined the other man's face. "Why would you want them to know? And why kill Marsh? We needed him."

He almost laughed at that one. *He* didn't need anyone. Perhaps this impotent has-been needed a half-dozen pathetic excuses for human beings rallied around him, but *he* needed nothing…no one.

"Marsh had served his purpose," he said simply.

The epiphany dawned, rather belatedly. A gasp echoed in the quiet. "You wanted them to know it was you?"

The smile that stretched across his face was answer enough.

"But why? If they know it's you…they'll—"

Dr. Waylon Galen stood, weary of the discussion. He moved behind his chair, in anticipation of exiting this unnecessary meeting. "They'll know their enemy is one they cannot defeat."

The other man's eyes widened perceptively. "You're not going to stop until you've destroyed them all."

Galen clapped his hands together three times, applauding the man's sudden ability to see what was right in front of his face. The reality that he was so close sent anticipation rushing through Galen's veins. "I've spent more than a decade underground. Working out of temporary labs in jungles. Moving from place to place to avoid detection. But no more. Now all that Center possesses will be mine. I was the one who created the Enforcers. They belong to me. That never changed."

"Why all the subterfuge?" The other man shook his head in bewilderment. "Thurlo? Archer? What was the point? I thought you needed the key code."

Galen leaned forward and braced his hands. "I only need one thing and that will be mine very soon. Money is power. You'll see. I need *her* or her replacement on my side."

"Why kill all those people at the hospital in Mexico where Justin Winters had been?" he demanded, his bravado peeking from behind his fear. "Did you think I wouldn't hear about that? Center is all over it. They know it was your doing."

Galen nodded, mentally chalking one up for his nemesis, O'Riley. "They seem to know a great deal." He had a feeling his ally here was playing both sides of the fence. Oh well, that wouldn't matter in the grand scheme of things. His destiny was already in place.

"I don't understand." He shook his head, his confusion clearly mounting.

"You don't need to understand," Galen assured him. He straightened and moved toward the door but hesitated before leaving. He shook his head and glanced back at his befuddled visitor. "Did O'Riley really think that I wouldn't find out he'd sent in an Enforcer? You've both greatly underestimated me. I wonder if either of you fully realizes what you have done." He didn't wait for an answer. He left. Nothing anyone could say at this point would slow the momentum.

Caroline Winters was doomed if she did not support him.

And so was the Collective either way.

"I SHOULD BE GOING," Caroline said to her host. "The reception was lovely. I had a wonderful time."

Dorothy Sizemore gave Caroline a brief hug. "Thanks for coming, Madam President." She drew back and winked. "I knew you wouldn't change."

Caroline couldn't help but smile. "I'm still the same person I was before the election."

Dorothy nodded. "Ambitious overachiever and the apple of her daddy's eye." Her expression turned somber then. "I know you still miss him."

Congressman Clayton Mattson had been a strong supporter of the school Caroline and her friend had attended. But more important than that, he had been a great father. One all her friends had admired.

"I do," Caroline admitted. She always would.

Dorothy curled her arms around one of Caroline's and tugged her nearer. "But my, my that husband of yours makes a fine replacement for the man in your life."

Caroline beamed. He did indeed. Her father would

like the way things were going for her and Justin. He had wanted more than anything else for his only child to be happy. And she was on her way, finally.

"Nobody move!"

The screamed threat came out of nowhere and seemed to be all around them at the same time.

Caroline searched the room, her gaze coming back to rest on her husband. Her breath evaporated in her lungs when her brain assimilated the fact that the man who had shouted those harsh words had a gun jammed into Justin's temple and an arm wrapped tightly around his throat.

Agent Levitt and three others were suddenly around her, backing her from the room.

"I said, don't move!" The man's furious gaze crashed into Caroline's where she watched between Levitt's and the other agent's broad shoulders.

"Stop," she ordered her security. She would not allow them to usher her from this room at the risk of Justin's safety.

"Ma'am," Levitt murmured, "we have to get you out of here."

"No. Not without Justin."

"The others are already formulating a strategy to rescue your husband but my orders are clear. Remove you from the threat at all costs."

Caroline refused to move. "I said no."

"I want her to see this!" the angry man who'd posed as a waiter screamed.

Caroline's heart dropped to her feet. Dear God. She

suddenly knew what he was going to do. He intended to kill Justin while she watched. How had he gotten past security?

"You have to stop him," she whispered to Levitt. "Don't you see what he's going to do?"

Levitt knew. He didn't have to say anything. Caroline felt the change in his posture…saw the tightening of his jaw. She heard him whisper three curt words that would echo from the communication device on his lapel into the earpieces of every Secret Service agent on site. "Take him out."

The events that unfolded next left Caroline paralyzed by a new kind of shock. Even moments afterward she would not be able to move or speak. She could only stand there, perfectly still, watching the scene play out over and over in her mind.

Justin spun in the man's hold, forcing the gun barrel upward in the same instant with his left hand. Not missing a beat he grabbed and twisted the man's head with his right. The sound of his neck snapping echoed in the deafening silence. The would-be killer crumpled to the floor. The guests shrieked and scrambled to move aside.

Agents suddenly swarmed around Justin.

"Let's get Freedom out of here."

Levitt's voice. He'd just ordered her evacuation from the premises. Freedom was her code name.

Before the haze of confusion could clear completely from her mind she'd been hustled into the waiting armored limo and whisked away.

"Justin," she murmured, at last finding her voice.

"Mr. Winters is fine, Madam President," Levitt assured her. "He's in vehicle number three directly behind us."

Caroline swiveled in her seat and stared out through the heavily tinted glass. The other vehicle was right behind her.

She settled back into the elegant leather, exhaustion clawing at her. She blinked and tried to rationalize what she had just witnessed. Justin had executed moves only a professional bodyguard…or trained killer…would be able to perform. She thought about that day in the parking lot behind the restaurant and how he'd prevented her from being shot. She'd excused that incident by telling herself he'd simply gotten lucky. Anyone could have pushed her out of the way if he'd seen the threat quickly enough. It hadn't taken any particular skill to do that, just a keen awareness of his surroundings. The fact that he'd recognized the threat before any of her security was just plain old luck.

But tonight had nothing to do with luck.

Thwarting that killer had been about expertise.

Expertise in the art of protection…in the science of killing.

Justin had killed that man in a split second with a move that no normal, untrained human would even know to make.

Justin Winters had never undergone any such training.

Justin had kept himself fit, but he possessed no particular physical endurance or courage. He would never have dreamed of killing another human, much less of acting without thought.

That only left one possibility.

The man who'd come back to her...brought her more pleasure in a few days than she had known in five years of marriage...was not the husband she had lost three months ago.

Chapter Nine

Caroline tugged the brush through her hair as she stared at her reflection in the large, beveled-glass mirror. She'd been standing here like this for more than half an hour, stroking her hair with the silver brush her mother had given her on her sixteenth birthday and peering at the woman she scarcely knew anymore. What had gotten her to this place where she could trust no one? Not even those closest to her.

Pretty soon he would knock on the door to the dressing room and ask if she was all right. And how would she answer that?

She couldn't possibly be all right.

She had no idea who the man posing as her husband really was. Laying the brush aside she closed her eyes. That was insane. Impossible. She swayed, then clutched the marble vanity top to steady herself. He looked like her husband. Talked like her husband. They had discussed numerous moments from their past. Admittedly there were things he didn't remember, but that went hand-in-hand with the injuries he had sustained in the plane crash. There was so much he did know. How could an impostor possibly know all those things?

If anyone ever found out that the thought had even occurred to her she would be carted away in a strait-jacket immediately. She doubted even Rupert would stand by her under those circumstances.

But she had seen Justin's uncharacteristic response to the danger. Had noticed the other, more subtle differences that were so un-Justin like. He certainly hadn't learned to kill people while he lay in a coma in that hospital.

Fury whipped through her, searing away the vulner-ability. She did not like this feeling. Being out of control was not the norm for her and the past several weeks had been all about no control at all.

It was time to stop the downward spiral. There was only one way for her to know the truth.

And it wouldn't wait a minute longer.

Tightening the sash of her robe she charged from the dressing room, slamming the door behind her.

Justin looked up as she entered the room. He set the book he'd been reading aside and stood. "Would you like a glass of wine?" He gestured to the bottle he'd opened and the two stemmed glasses waiting next to it.

"No," she said flatly. "I don't want any wine." She definitely needed to keep her head about her and not let her temper run away with her. She would not be seduced or distracted now. "I want the truth."

He turned his hands palm up and spread his fingers in an act of openness. "I'm not certain what you mean by that, but I can see that you're upset. It's understandable after what happened. Tell me what I can do."

She strode up to him and planted her hands on her hips. "It's simple, tell me who you are."

Cain had expected any number of questions, but not that particular one. He had anticipated her fear of sounding "nuts" would prevent her from going that route. Obviously he'd overestimated her vanity.

He reached for her, but she dodged his touch. "You know who I am," he said softly, ensuring that there was no accusation or condescension in his tone.

She shook her head slowly, deliberately. "Justin Winters knew nothing about aggressive self-defense. He was a pacifist of the highest order. Any excuse you offer for your actions tonight, however exemplary, won't be good enough."

Cain had known that question would come and had taken appropriate steps to protect his cover. "You're right."

One eyebrow lifted slightly higher than the other as surprise registered. She hadn't expected that.

"The old Justin had no idea how to protect himself, much less his wife," he said with exaggerated disgust. "I couldn't do anything but analyze and advise on computer systems and set up remote links. I wasn't a man…I was a coward."

Her expression softened the tiniest bit and her stance wavered a little. "You've—Justin was never a coward."

"Yes." He nodded adamantly. "I was. I didn't want to know the unpleasant side of life. I was raised in privilege, my partnership skyrocketed. I've never had to make my way in life in any respect." He looked away, forcing his eyes to water for effect. "Not until the crash."

He was winning the battle. She reached out to him, placed her hand on his shoulder in a comforting manner.

"I know it was difficult."

He stared at her hand a moment then took it in his own. "You have no idea. I thought I'd never see you again."

The way she looked at him then…the need and hurt simultaneously vying for her attention shifted something inside him. He suddenly hated the lie he'd just told her. Didn't want to hurt her this way—and it would hurt her. When she learned the truth…

He gritted his teeth and banished the thought. Whatever it took. Completing his mission was all that mattered. She would get over whatever hurt he wielded. At least she would be alive. She would surely be grateful for that.

"I still don't understand how you could have done what you did tonight," she said, a part of her still uncertain, unwilling to let the issue rest. Most of her anger had subsided.

"I didn't want to be helpless anymore. I've been practicing with Copeland now and then." He shrugged, knowing the gesture would come off as goofy, vulnerable. "I've only learned a few moves. Lucky for me one of them was exactly what I needed tonight."

She still looked suspicious, but only a little. "But you killed that man."

He nodded. "I know. It was…awful. I just reacted. I had no idea I would kill him." He pumped up the vulnerability in his eyes. "But the thought that he might hurt you…"

The last obliterated any remaining doubt she suffered.

"Justin, I'm sorry for making this worse." She pushed her arms around his waist and hugged him close. "I don't know what got into me. I think maybe I've been in a kind of shock, couldn't think clearly. I should have realized you were experiencing the same." She heaved a breath against his chest.

He slid his arms around her and closed his eyes, allowing the feel of her warm body pressed so near to his to have its usual effect. His muscles tightened and blood rushed to his loins, hardening his sex. Making him want her so badly he could barely draw in a breath. He didn't understand the insatiable hunger to know this feeling. He shouldn't permit it and yet…he couldn't resist.

IT WASN'T TOO LATE for this to be a special night. Caroline pulled free of his arms and smiled. The same desire she felt was reflected in those clear blue eyes. He wanted her. He really did. Justin had changed…wanted to make things work. She had to stop fighting him. She'd waited so long for this moment….

She drew him toward the bed and said softly, "I want to show you how much I trust you."

As he watched, she released the sash to her robe and

opened it wide. The cool silk skimmed down her body to pool around her feet like a puddle of pale-yellow sunlight.

His fingers tightened into fists of restraint as she reached for one flimsy strap and tugged it off her shoulder. Slowly, ever so slowly, she repeated the move with the other strap then dragged the gauzy material down her breasts, along her rib cage and over her hips.

She stood very still for a time, reveling in the way his gaze moved over her body. When she could wait no longer, she stepped out of the ring of sensuous fabric and moved toward him, swaying her hips provocatively as her hair slid over the swell of her breasts. Tiny, racy jade-colored panties were all that concealed any part of her now.

He was still dressed. She reached out and released the first button holding his shirt closed over that awesome chest. Then another and another, until the designer garment lay open, save for the tails that were still tucked into his trousers.

Her fingers more sure than she had expected, she tugged at the closure of his belt, then pulled it free. The hiss of leather gliding against silk made her shiver. She tossed it aside and unbuttoned his trousers. His shirttail pulled free with ease, and she pushed it over his shoulders, allowing her bare breasts to graze the warm flesh of his chest.

The sound of his ragged breathing filled her ears, made her quiver with renewed anticipation. He shook his arms free of the confining shirtsleeves and the pale-blue garment fell to the floor.

Moving away a step, she studied his well-defined chest and broad, broad shoulders. He was magnificent. Her gaze swept over those muscular arms, pausing briefly on the bandage, and she thought of the power he possessed…the strength to kill an enemy. The courage. Another shiver skittered over her naked skin.

Now, for the coup de grâce. She wanted him to know how very much she trusted him, no matter that she showed weakness from time to time. She was only human, just as he was. Their future was all that mattered. The children they would have. All of that waited in this new future together. He had made all the changes so far. It was time she compromised as well…allowed herself to be vulnerable—completely—to him.

Caroline dropped to her knees and removed his shoes, first one and then the other. She rolled off each sock and tossed it aside to join the shoes.

She reached up, her gaze colliding with his, as her fingers latched on to the zipper of his slacks and lowered it.

The intensity in those piercing blue eyes very nearly undid her. He looked more vulnerable than she would ever have imagined. So filled with need and desire. His neediness emboldened her…made her want to show him just how much pleasure she could bring him.

His trousers whispered along the length of his strong legs, down and off, to land somewhere on the floor on the other side of the room.

Her gaze moved upward once more and her breath caught at the bulge filling his briefs. She'd seen Justin in his briefs before…but never like this. Slowly, carefully, she pulled down the undergarment, eased it over his swollen sex, and down those long, sturdy legs. The briefs joined the trousers.

At last he was naked. Caroline sat back and gloried in the beauty of him. How could she have been married to this man for more than five years and never once seen him like this? They had wasted so much precious time. The feel of her damp feminine curls against the backs of her calves reminded her how very ready she was for this relationship to move forward. Not in all those years of marriage had she grown moist merely looking at him. She had done that over and over the past few days. Whenever they were alone together, whenever he spoke to her. The sound of his voice, no longer rough from disuse, made her want him.

If his jagged respiration was any indication, he wanted her just as much. That moment would come. But now, she had some catching up to do. She wanted to pleasure him the way he had her just the other night.

Uncertainty warred with her determination. This was something she had never done before…something private between a husband and wife…but her husband hadn't wanted his wife until now. It was well past time they shared this most intimate act.

She shifted her weight to her knees and touched him. He felt as hard and sleek as granite. Her breath hitched as he pulsed, hot and alive, in her hand. Her entire body tingled and quivered with excitement…with anticipation. She leaned forward and tasted him, just one little swipe of her tongue. Smooth…intoxicating. She wanted him to cry out as she had. She wanted him to lose control.

Strong hands abruptly slid beneath her arms and scooped her up and onto the bed. He came down on top of her, his eyes gleaming with primal need, his breath ragged spurts. She started to protest but he latched on to her breast. Sucked hard, savagely so. She whimpered, felt her feminine muscles spasm with the aftershock of his hot, drawing mouth. He licked and nibbled, his hips undulating against her, nudging her, not wanting to wait…like an animal, unable to control the reflex.

He moved lower, leaving a path of hot, damp flesh wherever his mouth lathed and suckled. He traced each rib with his tongue, dipped in and out of her belly button until she thought she would scream with the incredible feel of it.

On his knees between her legs, he sat back and stared at her nude body.

"Please," she murmured. "Don't make me wait."

He positioned himself, drawing a gasp from her. He felt so damned good. His hands went under her buttocks, lifted and pulled her toward him, sinking himself inside her inch by inch.

Her fingers fisted in the sheets. He stretched her to the limit…filled her to capacity and then some. When he sealed her intimate juncture against him completely, he held very still, his breathing a perfect match to her own rapid, shallow puffs.

He held her that way for a time, allowing her body to fully adjust to his invasion, the stretching sensation alone sending her closer and closer to that exquisite peak. Every beat of his heart made him pulse harder inside her.

He kissed her slowly, thoroughly, until tears welled in her eyes, until her whole world was spinning around her. She clutched at his strong back as reason fled, leaving only sensation…sensation after sensation. The feel of his heart pounding in his chest echoed her own.

This was right.

This was perfect.

Then he started to move. Every slide and thrust along her feminine walls added a new layer of pleasure to the cascade of pleasure stroking every nerve ending of her body. Lights flickered behind her lids. She wanted to share all that she felt with him, but her mind couldn't form the words. She could only feel and draw closer and closer to that edge of pure bliss.

His entire body tensed and she knew he was on the verge of release too. She lifted her hips to meet him. He cried out at the unexpected move. Faster, harder, she pushed, pumping her hips to meet his every thrust, squeezing him, until they came together. His body trembled with the burst of release…she cradled him, taking all of him deeply inside her.

He rolled onto his side, held her in his arms and fought to catch his breath. She struggled to capture hers as well. She pressed her face against his sweat-dampened chest and listened to his heart pound.

She would never survive losing him now.

Never.

CAIN LAY very still as his respiration and heart rate returned to normal. Image after image, sensation after sensation kept replaying in his mind, twisting in his gut. Her on her knees before him. The heat and near-violent responses of her body. Orgasm had shaken her, rippled through her muscles like nothing he'd ever experienced.

But nothing matched the feel of him buried deep inside her. So hot and tight…so welcoming. He wanted to sink himself there again. To stay joined with her all through the night.

When she'd brought him to the edge of climax she made him feel…emotion.

He'd never fully understood what it meant to care so deeply for someone that you would die for them. He would die for his mission…but the human factor had never before entered into the equation.

Wanting to protect her was no longer about the mission…it was about her. He had to protect her. He could not bear to see her hurt. He had known when he'd had to kill that man at the party that she would see him in a different light. The idea that she would hate him… wouldn't want him to touch her again almost drove him out of his mind.

He'd had the proper motivation for his actions tonight. Had managed to smooth over the situation, but none of that changed the way it left him feeling.

This was a failure, he recognized that. But he could not stop the alien feelings. He needed to protect her. To hold her close and destroy anyone or anything that threatened her. That made him unreliable in this mission. He should report the failure to O'Riley.

But he would not.

He could not.

He was the only one who could save her.

She slept in his arms, trusting. He'd wanted her trust. Now he had it. But he would never own her heart. Another man, a dead man, owned her heart.

He had never needed anyone to care about him before.

Confusion lined his brow. Perhaps he didn't really need anyone now. These bewildering feelings might be side effects of what they had just shared.

He'd never made love with a woman, not like that, until Caroline. He'd had sex before, but this had been different. He recognized that, knew how it had affected her. He had considered that the next time might not be so all-consuming…so powerful, but tonight had proven him wrong.

He had never been wrong before.

THEY'D FALLEN ASLEEP, exhausted, when the telephone rang.

Cain came alert first.

The tiny hitch in Caroline's breath told him that the second ring had startled her.

"I'll answer it," he said as he reached for the receiver on the bedside table.

"No!" She pulled at his arm. "Let the answering machine get it."

He studied her in the dim light. "What makes you afraid?"

She peered into his eyes, fear welling in hers. "The only person who has ever called me on this line is you."

The machine picked up on the fourth ring. The automated voice instructed the caller to leave a message after the beep.

"Caroline…"

Cain's gaze shot to the machine as he listened to the voice of Justin Winters speaking to his wife from the grave.

Chapter Ten

Center
Ghost Mountain
Final Countdown
Day 2

"Sir."

Director Richard O'Riley looked up to find his secretary, Clara, hovering in the door. He slipped the photo he'd been staring at back into the desk drawer where it belonged. The elegant silver frame with its accompanying photo of his lovely ex-wife had once held a position of honor on his desk. But no more. His life with Angela was over…had been for a while now. He didn't know why he punished himself by staring at her picture every time he had a few minutes alone in his office. It wasn't as though he was over the hill. Hell, he was only fifty-eight. He could have a social life…if he wanted.

"Sir?"

He snapped to attention, annoyance, mostly at himself making his tone sharp, "Yes."

"Mr. Dupree is on his way up. He just arrived back at Center."

O'Riley stood. "Tell him I'll meet him in Lab Three." He had a technician standing by to assist.

In the corridor outside his office, O'Riley walked straight to the bank of elevators. Inside the car he selected sublevel three. He pressed his thumb against the scanner to authorize entrance to the restricted sublevel. Center had six floors above ground and four below. The most important lab work was done on the four subterranean levels.

Once he exited the elevator car on sublevel three a retinal scan was required to get beyond the double doors marked Restricted Access.

The doors opened automatically. A laser scan ensured that only one person passed through on each retinal approval. As the doors whooshed closed behind him he strode along the wide corridor until he reached the door marked Lab Three. The lower levels, as did all of Center, operated on a private power system not connected to any outside sources. All telephone lines were operated from a secure satellite system.

O'Riley entered the lab and nodded in greeting to the technician standing by. "Is it here?" the tech asked.

O'Riley nodded again. "On its way down."

His timing perfect, Dupree breezed through the door, a sleek black briefcase attached to his wrist via a state-of-the-art titanium bracelet. The bracelet, if opened without proper authorization, contained an explosive that would detonate, annihilating anything within a half-dozen meters, including whatever the briefcase contained.

After releasing the briefcase and placing it on a steel lab table, Dupree removed the two items it contained.

The letter.

The second item was half of the necessary key.

O'Riley visually surveyed what appeared to be a blank page, except for one small icon placed neatly at the top right-hand corner. No wonder Adam hadn't remembered anything about the letter from the Judas Mission other than that it was important. There was nothing to remember except that icon.

As tiny and insignificant as the icon, a miniature keyhole, looked, it spoke volumes about the letter. The icon represented DNA-dependent access. In this case two different kinds of DNA were needed. The writer's, Joseph Marsh, and the receiver's, Dr. Daniel Archer. Marsh, a former head of department at Center was nothing but a traitor, one who was now dead. Dr. Daniel Archer, the scientist who'd brought the Enforcers to fruition, was also dead. He had died because Marsh had been a fool.

Dupree passed the small black box that served as a cooling device to the technician. The box contained a tube that held a sample of Joseph Marsh's blood. His DNA was the first half of the key. The tech had already retrieved a stored sample of Daniel Archer's DNA.

O'Riley, Dupree peering over his shoulder, watched as a single drop of each man's blood was allowed to touch the icon on the page. Five seconds later handwritten words magically appeared on the white sheet of paper.

Not authorized to view the contents, the lab tech immediately moved away from the table.

Taking his time, O'Riley read the letter twice. Marsh had recognized his mistake...too late. He had tried to warn Archer. Marsh had been double-crossed by...

The name, even after reading it the second time, stunned O'Riley.

"I can't believe it..." Dupree murmured, echoing O'Riley's very thought.

He carefully placed the letter into a plastic sleeve the tech had provided. The document would be placed in his personal safe inside his office.

Silence reigned as O'Riley, accompanied by Dupree, moved down the corridor and back through the double doors. O'Riley didn't speak until they had boarded the elevator and were moving upward.

"Get me an appointment with Redmond," he told Dupree. "I don't want this going through anyone else, not even my secretary. I'll meet him in D.C., someplace private."

Dupree swallowed hard. "You are talking about Vice President Redmond?" he asked for clarification.

"That's the one."

Dupree nodded. "All right." He paused, licked his lips nervously. "Sir, does this mean—?"

The doors slid open on O'Riley's floor.

"Just get me the appointment. Today." He stopped outside the car and held the door to prevent it from closing as he looked directly into Dupree's eyes. "We're running out of time. This train wreck is going to happen. We just have to be sure we're on the right side of the tracks when it does."

White House
Oval Office

CAROLINE WAITED as patiently as she could for Agent Copeland's analysis. She'd played the tape of what was supposed to be Justin's voice. As guilty as it made her feel where Rupert was concerned, she had told no one else. She had to keep this to herself this time. Had to get to the bottom of who was behind these taunting calls. Justin's sources had not gotten back to him yet. He'd insisted he would get to the bottom of the calls, but Caroline didn't want to wait. Putting the old-fashioned answering machine she'd borrowed from her father's study on her private line had felt like a surrender to the anxiety all these strange things going on in her life had prompted. Now she was glad she had.

Agent Copeland studied the answering machine a moment longer before he spoke. "Madam President." His gaze met Caroline's. "I have a friend in forensics over at Quantico. They've got every imaginable device for analyzing data of all sorts. Let me take this to him. Maybe he can determine if the voice has been somehow fabricated." He shrugged. "You know, pieced together using snippets of Mr. Winters' voice from interviews and what have you."

That sounded logical to Caroline. "I'd like that very much, Agent Copeland."

When he had placed the small machine in his briefcase she added, "It's not that I don't trust the regular channels. I simply want to keep this quiet until I have a better handle on what's going on."

He nodded. "I understand, Madam President. No one will know."

"Thank you, Agent Copeland."

Caroline watched him go. Her stomach knotted with anxiety. It was the right thing to do. She didn't know who she could trust anymore. If she told Rupert, he would insist that others be told. He simply didn't understand that she couldn't let any of them know until she had some answers.

Was the voice on the tape really her husband's?

If so, how had the perpetrators of this taunting nightmare accomplished their feat? She wanted answers. If she discovered that Redmond was somehow behind this...

Caroline took a deep breath and forced herself to calm. She wasn't sure what she would do. A full-blown White House scandal was the last thing she needed. But there were ways to handle the situation discreetly, she felt certain. Once she had her evidence she would seek out such a way. Redmond would lose in the end, one way or another.

But first she had to be sure.

She checked the time and then her calendar. Lunch with Supreme Court Justice Turner was next. Caroline had a feeling the elderly man intended to warn her that he planned to retire. Nominations for a replacement would need to be made and confirmation hearings set in motion. She'd asked Rupert to look into possible candidates.

Justin intended to spend the morning reviewing the plans he and his partners had instituted before his disappearance. She hoped that meant he looked forward to going back to advising part-time. He needed to put his professional life back together. There had to be a life after the White House. Caroline smiled when she thought of the way he'd walked her to her office after breakfast this morning and kissed her at the door. He'd promised to pop in before she met with her luncheon appointment.

She stared at her wedding ring and considered how thankful she was not only to have Justin back safe and sound but also for this complete turnaround in his attitude about their marriage. She was so happy. The one thing that would make her life utterly perfect was if she'd gotten pregnant last night.

It wasn't impossible, she realized as she quickly counted off the days since her last cycle. A wide smile tilted her lips upward. She could be the first president to bear a child while in office. Certainly none of her male counterparts could top that, she thought with a devilish grin.

She had no way of knowing how it would affect her popularity in the polls and she didn't care. She wanted children. She wanted to do what was right for the people of this country, the polls be damned. No matter what her advisors whined about, she would never be led by mere popularity polls. Re-election might go down the toilet but at least she would be able to sleep at night. Her only worry woulde whether or not she could count on her vice president during her down time. At this point she definitely could not.

She couldn't help wondering how many former presidents could say the same.

CAIN WATCHED Caroline via remote-controlled cameras he'd placed at strategic points in her office. Since he couldn't sit around her office, this was the next best thing. The office he'd chosen to use for now wasn't far from hers. He had memorized the location of all hidden doors and passages for the swiftest access. He also monitored the hall outside her office. If anyone he deemed suspicious even got close he was there in a heartbeat.

As he watched, the smile on her face told him she was remembering last night. Heat flooded him instantly and every muscle went rigid. Last night had changed him in some way that greatly disadvantaged his objectivity.

The joining of their bodies had completed him in a way he hadn't realized existed. Throughout his entire life, he had not realized that a part of him had been missing. Until last night.

He had no basis from which to form an assessment of how he would endure life at Center without her. Even after they had debriefed him and reverted his facial features to the way they once were, he wasn't sure he could forget. Perhaps he would need a memory wipe. Though he wasn't certain even that would do the job. She was a part of him now on levels he couldn't comprehend. She might just prove impossible to erase. She existed in his blood...in his very cells. Death might be the only way to forget...

Cain thought about that for a time and decided that death would likely be better than a lifetime without her. He felt certain Center would consider him damaged beyond repair at this point anyway. The decision probably would not be his to make.

He would hear from O'Riley today. This operation would end as soon as the identity of the traitor had been uncovered and the threat neutralized. Cain understood that the enemy would consider the situation out of control at this point. The assassin's every attempt had failed. New strategy would be put into place and the time frame escalated. Changes of this nature always ended in mistakes. Mistakes left crucial clues.

The enemy had lost already.

His secure cellular phone vibrated, drawing his attention away from Caroline. Cain quickly removed the pen from his pocket and gave it a twist. He set it on the desk in front of him and answered the call. The pen would emit a jamming signal that would prevent his conversation from being recorded in any way for three minutes.

"Yes."

When his voice had been analyzed and identified on the other end of the line, O'Riley said, "We have the letter."

Cain's pulse quickened. "How does that affect my mission?"

"For now, it remains the same. I have a meeting in D.C. this afternoon that may indicate otherwise."

Cain didn't ask for details about the appointment. If he needed to know, O'Riley would tell him. Still, since it would take place in D.C. he had to wonder if it involved someone close to Caroline. His instincts warned him that it did.

"I'll contact you with any change. Be advised that the enemy is someone who knows you well."

Cain frowned. No one outside Center knew him well. "Your warning is unclear."

"It's Waylon Galen," O'Riley said at last. "He's the one who orchestrated all of this."

For a moment that felt like an eternity Cain couldn't get past the name. Dr. Waylon Galen was the scientist who'd engineered Cain's genetic code. He was, in a manner of speaking, his creator.

But he was also the enemy.

"I understand," he said to the man he knew waited for assurance that further clarification was not in order.

Cain closed his phone and put it away. He disengaged the jamming device and tucked it into his pocket as he assessed the intelligence O'Riley had just provided.

Waylon Galen was the original scientist who had perfected the technique for manipulating genes. His methods had allowed for superior gene structuring during the crucial stages of development, thus allowing a genetically superior embryo to reach maturity.

Cain had been the first. Until Cain's twentieth year Galen had overseen his instruction. Dr. Daniel Archer had found fault with Galen's work and Center had agreed with his findings. Galen had been furious, refusing to acknowledge the error. He had walked away and had supposedly died. Cain had always wondered if Center had terminated him. Now, considering his sudden reappearance, Cain could only guess that he had expected just that and had disappeared to prevent Center from such an action.

Archer had revised the program to include emotional conditioning. The other Enforcers, far younger than Cain, had responded well to the change. Cain had not. His aggression and single-minded determination had limited his use. This mission had come to him only because there was no other alternative.

Now, at age thirty-nine, he fully understood the concept of emotion. Not only did he understand it, but he also felt it. Felt a deep sense of regret that his and Caroline's time together would soon end. Felt immensely pained at even the thought of never seeing her again. But he had no choice. Even if he had, she would be horrified when she learned the truth. He knew the way other humans reacted to what they considered to be different.

She would look at him and see a monster. Especially considering the lengths Center had gone to in order to fool her. She would hate Center and Cain.

That was precisely why she could never know.

The vast majority of Center's funding depended upon the president. Having her angered at their methods would be totally unacceptable. She could never know. If she did and she got in the way, she would have to be eliminated.

Cain would do anything to prevent that. Even if it meant never touching her again after this mission was complete. And that was precisely what would happen. Her husband would die yet again. She would be left to mourn his loss…only this time it would be more devastating.

She loved him in a different way than before.

Cain couldn't draw in a deep enough breath. It was true. She loved the man she thought he was. Loved him more deeply than she had her real husband. The damage would be much greater this time. Yet, it was a small price to pay for life, Cain considered.

Caroline Winters could never know that her continued approval of Center was all that kept her in office…all that guaranteed her continued good health.

Center didn't have to execute anyone publicly. Therein lay the beauty of their discreet methods. They had many other ways that would never be seen as anything other than the pitfalls of this imperfect existence.

One way or another, Cain had to see that Caroline did not fall victim to their needs.

The voice emanating from the telephone answering machine puzzled him. Galen's doing, he imagined, but he could not fathom the reasoning behind it unless it was to make Caroline look unstable, as, indeed, it had done before Cain's emergence as her lost husband. But why the continued taunting? There was no legitimate reason to continue.

Unless there was another agenda that no one had uncovered as of yet.

The voice was right. He had watched videos and listened to conversations involving Justin Winters enough to know the original when he heard it. But Justin was dead. Though his entire body had not been found, enough remains had been gathered by Center's recovery team to ascertain that he was indeed dead. He had been involved on some level with the threat against his wife. They simply had not determined the nature and extent just yet.

Poor Caroline. Cain watched her via his handheld monitor. She had no idea of the enemies that surrounded her or that she walked among them each day. She looked up from the papers on her desk and stared across the room, a smile tugging at the corners of her mouth. She was thinking of him again. Of him and last night.

Justin had betrayed her and so had he. Whatever pleasure he could give her during their short time together was all she would have from the man she called her husband.

Moisture stung Cain's eyes. He blinked to dispel the burning. Frowning he reached up, touched his face and was startled to find tears on his cheeks.

So this was what it felt like to cry…to mourn the loss of something that had never really been his.

Georgetown
Final Confirmation

THE RESTAURANT was off the beaten path by anyone's standards. There would be no chance of running into Capitol Hill cronies or any other federal employees on this side of town. That the interior was dark and leaning toward the sleazy side was all the better.

O'Riley made his way to the very back table where Redmond, definitely in disguise in jeans, T-shirt and baseball cap, waited.

"How did you ditch your faithful followers?" O'Riley asked out of genuine curiosity as he took a seat. Dupree had scanned a twenty-block radius around the rendezvous point using the latest in satellite thermal imaging and not a federal agent of any sort had followed Redmond to the restaurant. O'Riley had waited in the van until he had been assured he wasn't walking into a setup.

"They think I'm in a meeting. An aide is covering for me." He shrugged. "Besides, I have one or two on my security detail I can trust and who trust me."

"How nice," O'Riley offered dryly.

"Get to the point, O'Riley. Time is limited."

"I wanted you to be the first to know that we've officially cleared you of any involvement in the crash that almost killed Justin Winters."

Redmond glared at him with equal measures of disdain and disbelief. "What the hell are you talking about?"

O'Riley smiled. Unfortunately the vice president had no idea who he actually was. He knew only that he represented another of those shadowy organizations that kept their finger on the nation's political pulse.

"Actually, sir, you were our primary suspect when the president first started to encounter problems with her daily calendar as well as those annoying calls."

"Look." Redmond leaned closer, fury hardening the lines of his face. "I don't know what the hell you're talking about, but I had nothing to do with any of that. Hell, I thought she was trying to drag me into her dementia. That's why I denied seeing that frigging letter. I'm just trying to cope with an unhappy House and Senate. That's all."

O'Riley looked at him knowingly. "And you would be doing that by stirring trouble among the old school who don't believe a woman should ever have been elected."

Redmond's gaze narrowed. "I do what I have to do to survive. You'd do the same."

O'Riley shrugged. "Maybe. In any event, our main concern is a special project the president is getting ready to fund for the next fiscal year. We felt your involvement might have meant you intended to work against us. You do anything to slow that down and we would have a major problem."

"What the hell are you talking about? What special project?"

Redmond would never know that he'd just been a party to a fishing expedition. O'Riley had to confirm what he'd discovered in the letter before he acted. He had to be absolutely certain it was no trick by Galen. There was only one way to do that...*this way.* Redmond, however, did know a threat when he heard one. And that was a good thing. O'Riley wanted him to know that he meant business. Redmond had had his fingers in just enough dirty business to know better than to play the offended card by walking away without hearing the rest.

"Special Project Eugenics."

Redmond choked back a laugh. "You mean that genetic research project a group of scientists somewhere in Colorado are whining about?"

"That would be the one." And that would be the extent of Redmond's knowledge on the project. Only the president herself would know more. Even she didn't know everything. The Collective saw to that. Briefed her personally with a presentation that promised the kind of research that could eliminate catastrophic diseases altogether. And it was true. The only thing that wasn't covered was the defense part of their work. That part was secretly funded by the Pentagon. If the president ever found out and didn't like it, she'd simply have to take that up with her joint chiefs of staff. She would know more eventually... just not yet. Not until it became necessary, as it had with her predecessor.

"Well, you're talking to the wrong man," Redmond said with an amused chuckle. "She won't let me touch that project. She already has an advisor on that one."

He had to mean Winslow. It was his job to ensure that the president took care of their needs. He'd fallen down on that end with the previous administration. The Collective was counting on him to make sure that didn't happen this time.

"Well, Mr. Vice President," O'Riley began by way of ending the meeting, "I appreciate your time. We just wanted you to know that you had been cleared of suspicion. I'm sure our advisor has taken care of our needs."

Redmond slanted him a pointed look. "I guess you'd better be talking to that congressman you seem to think you have in your pocket. Because if you think Winslow is working for you, you're wrong. He's pushing for funding to be cut. Has a new project on the table, off the record, of course."

O'Riley resisted the urge to smack that smug look off his face. "I'm sure you're mistaken," he prodded, needing confirmation.

Redmond shook his head from side to side. "Oh, no. No way. She's reviewing the package right now. If Winslow has his way, it'll be buried in the next bill she signs off on. You've been had, my friend. He's been pushing this new project since the final months of the last administration."

"Thank you, sir." O'Riley stood. "I won't forget your cooperation."

For the first time since they met, Redmond offered his hand. "I'm always happy to provide assistance."

"I'll remember that."

O'Riley walked away.

He had his confirmation now.

Winslow was working with Galen.

The whole strategy to undermine the president's mental stability was an effort to sway her. She'd likely stood on her principles of supporting Center. When Winslow couldn't sway her, he'd opted to get her out of power, if only temporarily. Killing her husband and making her look unstable would do the trick. Obviously, Redmond was anyone's dog who would hunt with him. He would have rolled over for next to nothing. Winslow had known that and used it to his advantage.

The Collective would be out and the Concern, obviously headed by Galen, would be in.

How interesting.

Too bad it wasn't going to work.

Chapter Eleven

"It's the only right thing to do, Madam President."

Caroline considered Congressman Winslow a moment before she spoke. Something about him needled at her. He was a respected member of Congress, hailed from a conservative midwest state…and yet.

"Why don't you leave the reports with me and let me review them a little more closely," she offered, unwilling to commit without further consideration.

He nodded, however reluctantly. "Certainly." She didn't miss his lingering glance at the stack of reports in question. Obviously he did not want to leave the package.

Too bad.

She didn't make snap decisions. She and her closest advisors would need time. His continued pressure that she shift her support from one project to another didn't feel right. After five terms on the Hill he knew the way things worked around here. His impatience was simply out of hand.

Caroline stood, a blatant act of dismissal. "I'll have an answer for you first thing in the morning."

Winslow pushed to his feet and straightened the lapels of his obviously expensive suit. "I'll look forward to hearing from you, President Winters. Time is of the essence here. This funding proposal really needs to go through with tomorrow's congressional package."

As they walked to the door, he paused. "You know, your father tried to get this project off the ground more than a decade ago. Perhaps you should look back at his old personal files if they're still available."

When the door was closed behind Winslow, Caroline gave him twenty seconds to make his way along the corridor and out of sight. She jerked the door open and motioned for Agent Levitt to join her.

Her mother. She'd have to call her mother first.

What if she wasn't home?

Caroline rubbed at the pressure that had begun in the center of her forehead. She had to be home. If she wasn't, Caroline knew where the spare key was kept.

"Yes, Madam President?" Levitt waited expectantly for her orders.

Why waste the time? Her father's files were stored in a closet in his office. Some of the older ones might have been relocated to the attic, but those from the last few years would still be downstairs where Caroline had put them. Her mother wouldn't have moved anything without mentioning it. She had to see those files. Winslow had purposely dropped that little tidbit. She wanted to know if he would be so bold as to lie.

After a quick check with her secretary to see that her schedule for the remainder of the afternoon was clearable, Caroline turned her attention to Agent Levitt who waited patiently.

"I need to go to my mother's home in Bethesda. Can you arrange that in the next few minutes?"

Levitt nodded. "Right away, ma'am."

The agent was already murmuring orders into his communications link as he left her office. Caroline had never been more thankful for his ability to react on a moment's notice.

After clearing her desk, Caroline gathered her purse and placed the reports Winslow had left in her briefcase and started toward the door. It opened just as she reached it.

"Oh." She pressed her hand to her throat, startled. "Justin, I need to make a quick trip to Mother's. Do you want to come along?"

"I'd love to." He reached for the briefcase. "Let me help you with that."

Glad to relinquish the heavy bag she smiled. "Thanks."

The trip to her childhood home took only a few minutes, considering they had missed the worst of the evening rush-hour traffic. The front car pulled to the curb, leaving the drive open for the SUV in which Caroline rode. A third vehicle parked behind the first along the curb in front of the classic colonial two-story.

Lora Mattson met Caroline and her entourage at the door. Levitt and two men entered the home first and ensured that all was clear while Caroline, her mother and Justin waited in the entry hall with two other agents.

"I'll never get used to this, Caroline," her mother

said. "It was bad enough with your father's minimal security detail."

"Sorry." Caroline kissed her mother's cheek. "I hope I haven't showed up at a bad time."

"Having you drop by is never a problem." Lora hugged Justin. The gesture appeared to startle him. "It's good to see you, Justin." She beamed a smile up at him. "I'm so thankful you're all right."

Lora Mattson rarely ventured into D.C. anymore. Her visits to the White House were even more rare. It wasn't that she wasn't proud of her daughter's accomplishment, but she still resented that politics had taken her husband from her. Caroline felt certain that was the same reason she'd never pursued a relationship with Rupert. She didn't want to fall in love with another man whose mistress was Capitol Hill.

Usually they kept in touch by phone or Caroline dropped by. But lately that had been far too infrequently. Emotion welled in her as she regarded her mother's aging beauty. As much as she loved her mother and didn't want to lose her, it was the natural cycle of life. Sometimes she wondered about the projects they funded. Was the constant search for eternal good health really worth the cost? Was it even meant to be?

Pushing aside the uncharacteristically somber thoughts, Caroline smiled brightly for her mother. "Mother, make us some of your Earl Grey while I prowl around in father's old files."

"Madam President," Levitt approached, "the house is clear."

Lora Mattson rolled her eyes. "Well, I could have told you that."

Caroline had to laugh. Her mother would never get it. Maybe she was better off that way.

Lora disappeared in the direction of the kitchen and Caroline and Justin went straight to her father's study.

The moment she opened the intricately carved wooden doors her father's essence assailed her senses. It still smelled like him. Every stick of furniture, every carefully selected piece of art represented the man who had once held court in this room.

The massive wood desk remained just as he'd left it. The final papers he had reviewed were still spread across his blotter pad. The pen he'd used to sign a piece of correspondence lay across one page in particular.

Other than the occasional dusting, no one ever came into this room. Her mother didn't want it disturbed. She tolerated Caroline's plundering because her father wouldn't have wanted it any other way.

Justin placed the briefcase in a chair. "What are we looking for?"

Caroline went to the closet on the far side of the room. "His files from those past couple of years before…" Before he died, she didn't bother to say. Justin knew what she meant. Several boxes were stacked on the floor. A fine layer of dust covered them. It had been a while since she had gone on a scavenger hunt.

She lugged out a box, Justin followed with two. As they set the boxes on the floor and dropped down next to them she considered her husband for a moment. He didn't appear to have any lingering problems from the crash...well, discounting his lapses in memory. But everyone had those from time to time. What really fascinated her was how quickly the scars faded. The ones on his back were scarcely visible anymore and the one on his face was barely there as well. You would never know he had been shot just days ago. He still wore a bandage, but he never complained about it.

Maybe her mind had exaggerated the damage when she'd first seen him. She had, after all, been in a sort of shock. Shrugging off the thought, she focused on the dozens upon dozens of manila folders. Each contained some report or project or grant that her father had reviewed respective to his work.

"Do you have a subject?" Justin asked as he opened one of the boxes closest to him.

Caroline reached for the briefcase and pulled the reports from inside it. After scanning the cover page of one, she said, "Look for Project Genesis."

Cain thumbed through the files, careful not to show any outward indication of the uneasiness gushing through him. Project Genesis was the original name for Project Eugenics. The Collective had restructured the program, starting with a new name after Dr. Galen had left.

Why would Caroline want information on Genesis? Why would her father have even had any dealings with Genesis? To Cain's knowledge it had been defunct for over a decade. His gut clenched in warning. This had something to do with her meeting with Winslow. He hadn't been able to listen in on the conversation; apparently Winslow had had himself some sort of jammer as well. But Cain had watched. He'd noted subtle changes in Caroline's posture and facial expressions during the course of the meeting. She hadn't liked what she was hearing.

Cain scrubbed a hand over his chin. He would have to get word to O'Riley. Winslow might be playing both sides. Cain couldn't make an accusation of that caliber without evidence. Winslow was the head of the Collective. Questioning his integrity could be seen as treason. Yet, Cain had no choice but to report what he had seen as well as what he suspected based on gut instinct.

His instincts rarely failed him.

"Here we go." Caroline pulled a thick file from the box she'd been sifting through. "Genesis." She took the file as well as the report Winslow had left with her and moved to her father's desk. She glanced up then. "This may take a while, Justin. Do you want to have tea with mother while I read through this?"

He nodded, his attention riveted to the folder. "Sure." He needed to know what was in that folder. By delving into the past she might very well be endangering herself without realizing it. He had to…stop it somehow.

"I'll just put these boxes away."

"Thanks," she murmured distractedly, already deeply focused on the pages in front of her.

Cain placed the boxes back in the closet, ensuring that the one that had held the file she'd taken was on top. The storage closet consisted of rows of shelves where boxes of files, books and other mementos of her father's professional life were stored.

As he left her father's study, Caroline's head remained bent over the file. Cain didn't bother to say anything. He was far too preoccupied himself. He had to know the contents of those pages.

In the entry hall Agent Levitt and two more of his men loitered, waiting for word from their commander in chief. Cain nodded an acknowledgment and continued through the house toward the kitchen. As a part of his preparations he had studied the floor plan of her childhood home in the event he might end up here. Another thing he hadn't understood until recently was the human need to cling to one another, to maintain close ties.

His only connections were to his peers at Center, the other Enforcers. But that was different...professional not personal. This was deeply personal. It was something he had just come to understand...had just scratched the surface actually.

Mrs. Mattson was pouring hot water into a silver teapot as Cain entered the kitchen. She looked up and smiled. He returned the gesture.

Caroline resembled her mother. Both had the same hazel eyes. Age had turned the mother's dark hair silver. Physically she looked in excellent condition for a woman beyond the age of sixty.

"Is she buried in a file already?" Lora sighed as she fretted with the china cups and silver spoons. "She always did dive into whatever she had on her mind." She looked directly at Cain then. "Just like her father. It's easy to be forgotten when your spouse is busy seeing after the whole nation."

Her eyes glimmered with emotion. Cain recognized the reaction as tears. Another of his own new acquaintances. She missed her husband…missed her daughter who had little time for her these days.

Cain read the feelings as easily as if she'd spoken them out loud. "She loves you," he said, knowing those were the words she wanted to hear. Her need was palpable.

Lora Mattson swiped at her eyes. "Oh, I'm getting foolish in my old age. Of course, she loves me." She offered the tray to him. "Just like she loves you."

He blinked, startled for the second time today as he accepted the tray.

Caroline's mother sighed wistfully. "Honestly, Justin, having you back has made all the difference. She looks happier than I've ever seen her."

He nodded, uncertain of what he should say in return. Uncertain of his voice.

She leaned close to him as she led the way back to the long entry hall. "Maybe this happy reunion will give me the grandchild I've always wanted."

The tray shook in his hands and Lora Mattson winked at him as if understanding his uneasiness.

Child.

He hadn't considered that kind of complication. He hadn't given any thought to what would happen after the mission other than the certainty he would never be allowed to see Caroline again.

Unprotected sex.

That's what their lovemaking had been. Whether or not she utilized any sort of birth control was not a part of the operation's profile. He couldn't help wondering then how Center would react to such a breach. And it would be a breach of protocol if not security.

Center owned him.

They would own his offspring.

To his knowledge there was no protocol for breeding among Enforcers.

Yet another new dilemma to ponder.

While Lora Mattson served the tea to her daughter in her father's study, and to the restless agents standing by, Cain experienced a whole new emotion.

Fear.

If Caroline Winters were to become with child as a result of their joining, her life as well as the child's would no longer be her own.

Her life would be worthless now if he learned that she and Winslow were plotting to overthrow the Collective.

Every finely honed instinct he possessed warned that he needed to brace himself for that inevitability.

For the next hour while Caroline remained trans-fixed by the Winslow report and her father's file, Lora Mattson gave Cain a guided tour of her daughter's life via family photos.

"I know you've heard all this before," she had wor-ried, clearly delighted at the prospect of boasting about her daughter's exploits as well as her accomplishments.

"I'm happy to hear it again," he had asserted.

Cain studied the photographs of Caroline as a child,

then as a blossoming young woman. Her beauty amazed him. Everything about her appealed to him. Seeing her barefoot in the sand on a beach or in cap and gown at graduation he longed to share those kinds of moments with her. He wished he could feel the sand between his toes…feel the sun on his face…while holding her in his arms.

But that was impossible.

He jerked from the fantasy and forced himself to think rationally. He couldn't let these emotions control him. He was far stronger than that. The sensations might be new to him, but he would conquer them.

His gaze sought and settled on the picture of Caroline.

He had no choice.

THOUGH HER FATHER'S files had backed up Winslow's assertions, Caroline still felt uncomfortable with the situation. Perhaps she would look at them once more in the morning before calling Winslow.

She looked at her husband's profile in the dim light of the SUV's interior as they journeyed back to the White House. He took her breath away. He was so very handsome. The way he could make her feel with a mere look…a simple touch. She sighed. Heat swirled low and deep in her belly.

He assisted her from the car and then carried the briefcase for her as they ascended the stairs to their room. She hoped tonight would be a repeat of last night. Her skin tingled at the possibility. Even the idea sent ripples of longing through her. It was true that she'd desired him all those years ago when they'd dated. She had begged him to love her this way when they were first married. But none of that compared to what she felt now.

The need—the urge—to be with him was an ache in her soul…a desperate longing.

She would never survive losing him again. That was a certainty. Now she understood why her mother still clung to her father's memory even after more than ten years. When a woman loved a man that much, it transcended death.

When they reached the presidential bedroom, Justin opened the door and waited for her to enter before him. He tossed the briefcase into a chair and shrugged out of his jacket.

"I was thinking," he said, his voice low, soft and incredibly sexy. "We could have some wine and then…"

The way he allowed the words to trail off made her entire body spasm with longing. She backed toward the en suite bath. "I think I'll shower."

He licked his lips, those piercing eyes devouring her. "I'll get the wine and then I'll dry your back."

She nodded, her throat closed with want.

Caroline stripped her clothes off, her fingers fumbling in their haste. Slacks, blouse, shoes, trouser socks, it all landed in a heap on the bathroom floor. She kicked the pile aside and turned on the shower to give the water time to warm. As she gathered towels she remembered the sexy pink gown she'd bought years ago and never worn. She quickly retrieved it from her bureau drawer and rushed back into the bathroom. She pressed the filmy fabric to her face and inhaled deeply. The scent of roses made her grateful that she'd kept the fragrant petals stashed in her special-occasion lingerie drawer.

She slipped beneath the warm spray of water and allowed the liquid heat to relax and soothe her muscles. As she shampooed her hair she thought of the way Justin had made love to her.

She hurried through the cleansing ritual and quickly towel-dried her hair rather than using the blow-dryer. She just couldn't wait to be with him. A swift swab of her skin with the towel and she slipped into the slinky gown. Narrow spaghetti straps held the silky fabric up. Its hem scarcely skimmed the tops of her thighs. She shivered as she tugged on matching lacy panties.

On second thought she snagged the dryer and removed most of the moisture from her hair. It was a little too drippy for the look she had in mind.

A little lipgloss and she was ready to spend a night of bliss in her husband's arms. Her mouth already watering for the taste of his, she slipped into the bedroom to join him.

She drew up short as her brain identified what she saw. He had the file and the report from the briefcase spread across the writing desk. With a glass of wine in one hand, he turned page after page, scanning each like a speed-reader. No, not a speed-reader—like a laser scanner. No one could read that fast.

"What're you doing?"

He looked up at her, his expression showing no sign of surprise or guilt. "Trying to figure out what you found so fascinating about this stuff." He flipped over another page and then stepped away from the desk as if he'd suddenly lost interest.

"Those documents are classified." Well, at least Winslow's report was. Her father's files were no longer sensitive. At least not to her knowledge.

He shrugged. "Sorry. I didn't realize. You didn't have them locked up or anything."

He was right about that. She'd left the material in plain sight. A frown worked its way across her brow. Why was she making such a big deal out of it? This was Justin. She trusted him.

In all the years they had been together she had never known him to invade her privacy in any way. He was an intensely private man. A breach of professional trust would have been unthinkable...but then he wasn't that Justin anymore. The accident had changed him.

Maybe he'd simply been bored.

She was blowing this out of proportion.

Seemingly oblivious to her inner struggle, he poured her a glass of wine and brought it to her. His gaze swept down her body and then back up, making her quiver.

"You look beautiful."

Caroline cleared her mind of all else. This was her husband. She would not let a foolish moment of curiosity ruin what they were building. With all that she had on her plate right now, worrying about the threats on her life and dealing with those taunting phone calls, she didn't need to borrow any more trouble.

She sipped her wine. "You don't look so bad yourself, Mr. Winters." She cocked her head and surveyed him as he had done her. "Maybe a little overdressed."

He smiled, and all other thought flew out of her mind. "Well, let's see what we can do about that."

That night when they slept he held her so tightly she could hardly breathe until they had both drifted off to sleep. Caroline didn't understand what had happened.

She would never know how making love to her had broken down the barriers he'd built...the severe control he'd kept all those years. Or how he had just learned that though intelligence and strength could be genetically engineered, emotions would not be conquered by mere cell manipulation.

Some things were simply intrinsic to humans and he was, after all, human.

Chapter Twelve

Intelligence Analyst Dupree along with a technician from Lab Three were on their way to D.C. to pick up the page Cain had taken from Caroline's father's file early that morning. They would analyze the page and determine if it was authentic to the time frame it supposedly represented.

Cain had quoted the contents of Winslow's report and the Mattson file verbatim to O'Riley. The reception on the other end of the line was not good. The director didn't have to spell it out. The evidence was damning. If Caroline went along with Winslow's proposal she would, in effect, be turning over the operation of Center to the enemy.

She couldn't possibly understand the ramifications. All presidents depended upon others to advise them on such matters. The steps she had taken thus far were no

different than anyone else's. But her innocence of
wrongdoing would not protect her any more than it had
protected those before her who had been eliminated.
Man had always cut out from among his midst any that
went against his beliefs. It was the way of the warrior.
Survival of the fittest.

It would always be that way.

If Caroline gave Winslow the go-ahead, she would
be eliminated.

Cain had been given the order to proceed immediately upon her authorization of support.

He would not survive the operation and the assassination would be chalked up to the plane crash. An undiagnosed brain tumor would be blamed for his
unexpected psychotic break.

He stood in the middle of the office he used to monitor Caroline's activities unable to move or speak. A
dozen scenarios reeled through his mind. Possible ways
that he could somehow right this wrong. But there was
no way. Everything depended upon Caroline. Telling
her would not work since she would think he had lost
his mind and would certainly summon security.

There was nothing he could do but wait.

He stared at the monitor that displayed her every
move, her smile. Her mother would be devastated by the
loss. The country would grieve as well. Others would
carry on, ensuring that their needs were met by elimi-
nating any and all obstacles from their path.

Cain threw the cellular phone in his hand across the
room, shattering it against the far wall. Rage coursed

through his veins. *Not right.* The two words echoed over and over again in his brain. *Not right. Not right.*

"Is everything all right, sir?"

Cain's gaze slid to the partially open door and the Secret Service agent who'd poked his head into the office.

"Go away," he growled, the ferocity of his words sending a lethal warning.

The agent nodded stiffly. "Yes, sir."

Already it had begun. When the killing was done the agent would remember the shattered phone on the floor and the deranged expression he'd seen on Justin Winters' face. He would repeat the two simple words that had been uttered with animalian ferocity. And he would shake his head and wonder why he hadn't realized that something was very wrong.

Justin Winters hadn't been right since surviving the crash and subsequent coma. Somebody should have noticed. Someone should have stopped him.

But that was impossible.

His mission was ordained by the Collective.

Nothing could stop it from being carried out.

If he failed for some reason or refused to finish the job, they would only send someone else or perhaps simply allow the threat already looming over her to find fruition. Either way Cain would die as well.

The thought of dying evoked no reaction in him. But the mere idea of Caroline being hurt pierced him like a sword. Cut off his ability to breathe. Anguish curled and knotted inside him until he had to resist the urge to double over with the pain of it.

He searched for that neutral place he'd once possessed. That place of nothingness where he performed without regret or consideration of consequence. It was gone now. Banished by the woman who had reached deep inside him and touched his heart, bringing it to life in a way that he had not known existed.

On the monitor Caroline's secretary entered her office. Cain eased closer, listening carefully to the audio, which had failed him yesterday during Winslow's visit. He knew for certain now that the cagey bastard had used a jamming device. Probably one designed by Center like that Cain himself carried.

"File these documents as appropriate," Caroline instructed, "and call Congressman Winslow for me and let him know I'd like to meet with him to discuss moving forward on his proposal."

The secretary took the documents and left the office assuring the president that she would take care of it right away.

Cain's fingers clenched as the cold hard reality stabbed deep into his chest.

He had his orders.

There was nothing else he could do.

CAROLINE LOOKED UP as her husband entered her office. She couldn't help smiling. She did so love to watch him move. A blush heated her skin as she thought of all the ways they had made love the past few nights. She hadn't thought it possible to reach that level of blissful exhaustion.

"Are you planning to join us for lunch?" She glanced

at her schedule. "I know how much you love those fine gentlemen from the oil industry."

Two representatives of the American Oil Association had finagled a luncheon with the president in hopes of garnering support for their cause. Caroline had her own ideas about a few things the oil producers needed to do, but everyone knew that the black roots of oil ran deep in the White House soil. She wasn't foolish enough to believe she could ignore them. Whatever decisions she made, she would give them an audience just as she did others on many, many matters that affected this great nation.

She frowned. "Are you all right, Justin?"

He moved silently toward her, his expression tight with what looked like pain.

She met him halfway, taking his hands in hers and surveying him for visible signs of whatever was causing him such obvious discomfort.

"Please," she urged when he remained silent. "Tell me what's wrong."

He pulled free of her hands and lifted his to cup her face. The muscles of his throat worked as he fought to swallow or speak. Dear God, she didn't want to think what had happened to put him in this sort of agony.

His eyes never leaving hers, he slowly lowered his mouth until it closed firmly over hers. In that final second before her eyes closed she was certain she saw tears in his.

He kissed her, tenderly at first, then harder. His fingers slid down to curl around her throat. He drew her nearer, his fingers tightening to an almost painful grip. But she wasn't afraid. Not in the least.

"I love you," she murmured between kisses.

His fingers abruptly relaxed and he pulled away from her. Startled she peered up into his eyes to find them wide with uncertainty…something along those lines.

"I have to go."

"Justin!" she called after him, but he didn't look back, just kept walking until he was out of her office. She moved to the door and watched him disappear down the corridor. Her fingers went to her throat where her skin still burned from his punishing grip.

Whatever had happened to upset him like this had to be connected to the accident. Somehow she had to convince him to have that follow-up physical. There could be underlying trouble that had gone undiagnosed.

Her telephone rang and she moved back to her desk. Putting the worrisome thoughts aside, she pressed the intercom button.

"Madam President, a Special Agent Marvin Shaw is on line one for you. He represents Quantico's forensics department."

Agent Copeland's friend. "Thank you, Barbara."

Caroline quickly picked up the receiver and pressed the button for line one. "Hello, Agent Shaw."

"Good afternoon, Madam President. I have the results of your voice analysis."

"Thank you, Agent Shaw. I really appreciate your taking the time to do this." Now she would know if the voice that kept taunting her was really Justin's and maybe some insight as to how someone had devised the calls, since her husband certainly hadn't made them.

"Let me say it's a pleasure to be of service to you, ma'am. Please feel free to call upon me anytime."

Caroline struggled to put the disturbing incident with Justin aside and settled into her chair. "I'll remember that, Agent Shaw. What were your conclusions regarding the recording?"

"Well, ma'am, I don't know how this came about. But the voice on the recording is definitely a match to the samples you provided of your husband's voice."

Shock radiated through Caroline. Agent Copeland had provided a couple of recordings of Justin's interviews before the crash.

"You're sure about that?" She hadn't really expected that analysis. She'd expected to learn it was a fake in either content or development.

"Yes, Madam President, I'm positive."

"Then someone doctored it. Created the recording from bits and pieces retrieved from recordings of his voice." Justin had been recorded in various settings. In interviews as the spouse of a presidential candidate and then as the First Husband. He'd played that one to the hilt. That didn't even include his work. He was always traveling around doing speeches in one capacity or another.

"President Winters, I'm afraid this is no doctored recording. This is the real McCoy. Mr. Winters' voice sounds a bit slurred at times. The slur pattern is consistent with intoxication or medicated levels where speech is impaired. But there is no question as to whose voice is on the recording. Every marker is a match. Every last one."

"Thank you, Agent Shaw. I appreciate your help."

Caroline didn't actually remember ending the call. But the receiver made its way back to the cradle so she must have. She stood there for a long time unable to form a coherent thought.

Why would Justin make those recordings and have someone play them to taunt her? It didn't make sense. What did he hope to accomplish? And what about the agent's words about the slur pattern of the voice indicating intoxication or perhaps a certain level of medication?

The hospital. He'd made those calls from the hospital. She was sure of it. Maybe not of his own free will. Obviously whoever else was involved still intended to go through with whatever crazy scheme he'd originally concocted.

Caroline buzzed her secretary. "Get me the administrator of that hospital where Mr. Winters was discovered. I need to speak with him immediately."

"Right away, President Winters."

Two minutes later her phone buzzed. "The hospital administrator is standing by," Barbara announced.

Caroline quickly snatched up the phone. "Mr. Ramirez," she said breathlessly, "I apologize for having to bother you but—"

"Madam President, this is Senor Garcia. I am the acting administrator."

Worry furrowed across her forehead. "I need to speak with Mr. Ramirez," she urged. "It's urgent."

"I'm afraid that is most impossible, madam. Mr. Ramirez is dead."

Shock reverberated through her. "I'm sorry to hear that." She moistened her lips. She had to speak to someone who had taken care of her husband. "Perhaps I could speak with Dr. Hernandez. He was in charge of my husband's care—"

"Dr. Hernandez is dead as well."

Ice slid through Caroline's veins. Desperation surged. "There…there was a nurse. I can't remember her name but she—"

"Madam, there is no one to talk to regarding your husband's stay here." He fell silent a moment. During that infinitesimal space in time Caroline's knees went weak beneath her and she had to sit.

"They are all dead, Madam President," Mr. Garcia went on solemnly. "Murdered. The police are still investigating the matter. Your husband's medical file was taken. An investigator from your country came, but he did not share his conclusions."

An investigator? "Do you remember the investigator's name?" Her heart stumbled with anticipation…or maybe fear.

"I am sorry, madam, I do not recall."

Caroline ended the call, then dropped the phone back into place. She struggled to draw in air.

They were all dead.

The voice in the recording was Justin.

Someone from the U.S. had gone down and looked into the murders. But who? Why had no one told her what happened?

She clasped her icy fingers together and tried to think of what to do.

All the little inconsistencies she'd noted in Justin's behavior suddenly whirled inside her head. His passionate lovemaking. Her unexpected attraction to him from the moment he returned from the dead, when those feelings toward him had long ago died.

This couldn't be happening.

She needed help.

She started to get up but hesitated. She reached for the phone and then stilled. Her every move, her every word was being monitored for the sake of national security…for posterity.

She had to get out of here.

Had to call someone…Dennis.

He would know what to do.

Caroline grabbed her purse and rushed to the executive washroom. She closed herself in one of the stalls, knowing her privacy would not be invaded there, and entered Dennis's private number.

He picked up on the third ring.

"Are you in the middle of a session?" She swiped at the tears rolling down her cheeks. Dammit. She did so hate to cry. Presidents weren't supposed to cry unless national tragedy struck. A mere marital problem didn't count. But this…this was so much more than that. With every fiber of her being she understood that.

She heard the muffled sound of her friend's voice as he asked that whoever was in the room excuse him for a moment. She heard him get up and then a few seconds later a door closed.

"What's up, Caroline?"

"I'm sorry to bother you in the middle of the day," she said, her voice quavering. In less than an hour she had a luncheon engagement. A Secret Service agent likely waited outside the door. She was supposed to meet with Winslow again. But she had to know what this meant…the recording…the murders…

"Don't worry about it. Tell me what's going on. Has something else happened? You haven't been shot at again, have you?" He chuckled in an attempt to inject some humor into the moment. "You sound like you're in a well."

She huddled her free hand around her mouth as she spoke, not wanting anyone else to hear. "The calls…it was Justin."

Silence.

"Quantico did a voice analysis. It's him. No question. And there have been all these other little changes like—"

"Like his sudden about-face where his sexuality was concerned," Dennis guessed.

Caroline nodded, a sob tearing at her chest. "I don't know what to do. Last night I even found him looking at some of my reports. He's never done anything like that before. I'm not afraid of him," she hastened to add. "But something is wrong and he refuses to seek additional medical care."

She started to shake. First her arms and legs and then her torso.

"Okay. We need an intervention here, babe. He's—"

"Oh, God." Nausea roiled. "The hospital. They're all dead," she told him, hysteria rising. "The doctor, the nurse, the administrator. Anyone who had anything to do with his care in that Mexican hospital is dead. And his file is missing."

"Holy cow." The words were a hiss of breath. "Caroline, I'll tell you straight up that I noticed a few differences myself, but I rationalized them away. It was so easy. With the crash and the coma. But something's wrong here. Very wrong. You've got to get him confined until you can get to the bottom of the situation."

"Confined?" She clutched the phone in an effort to still her shaking hands. "What do you mean? Like committed?"

"No, no. Nothing nearly so dramatic as that. The press would have a field day with it. Tell your security supervisor that you suspect something is out of sync. Have them hold Justin in your suite of rooms until you can have him evaluated. Hell, I'll come over there and do the mental evaluation myself. Get one of those generals over at Walter Reed who has nothing else to do to pop over there pronto and do the physical. Meanwhile get the CIA and FBI or one of those three-letter agencies down to Mexico. This is all wrong. Hell, babe, you know what to do."

Caroline moistened her lips. He was right. She did know what to do. "The temporary administrator said someone had already been there." How could that be?

Surely she would know about it? The CIA briefed her every morning. And what the hell was she doing cowering in a bathroom stall with this insanity going down around her? Determination seared through her and she pushed out of the stall.

Some part of her realized that this new vulnerability was associated with the intensity of her physical relationship with Justin—she was still finding her balance there—as well as with his sudden resurrection from the dead.

But she had to be strong now, had to do what she did best. Take charge.

"How soon can you get here, Dennis?"

She dampened a paper towel and cleaned up her face.

"It'll be later this evening. I'm scheduled straight through until seven. Unless you think I should come now. I can cancel—"

"No." She shook her head in punctuation of the word. "Come when you're finished for the day. I'll tell the service staff you're coming for dinner. You've been here before. No one will think anything of that." The other necessary steps she would need to take ticked off one by one in her head. She would get this done. Protect Justin from himself or whoever was involved in this.

"Be careful, Caroline," Dennis warned before disconnecting. "If he's unstable he could hurt you."

Her hand went instinctively to her throat…

CAIN WATCHED on the monitor as Caroline came back into her office. He'd paced the halls since walking away from her. He hadn't been able to follow his orders. He couldn't bring himself to hurt her. And now he had only two choices. He could call O'Riley and tell him that he should be replaced or he could take Caroline and run.

The latter was the only way to ensure her safety.

Since there was no way he could walk away and leave her to face certain death, running was the only real option.

All he had to do was get her out of this building.

Once free of these walls, no one could touch him.

He was too good at evasion. His training was far too extensive for the most highly trained security personnel even to come close.

Cain considered the items he would need. A weapon and a secure cellular phone, both of which could be gotten from any one of the agents on Caroline's security detail. He only needed to disable one of them.

He took the corridor that would lead to their bedroom suite. He would snag an agent en route and leave him in the room to regain consciousness.

"Justin."

The sound of Caroline's voice made him hesitate. It startled him that he hadn't sensed her presence. Was he so focused that he hadn't felt her come up behind him? Or were those alien emotions controlling more than his heart?

"I'm sorry, Justin, but this is the only way."

Before her words fully assimilated in his brain, four agents had surrounded him. He took two down in as many seconds. When he went for the third, a weapon readied for firing, the sound echoing around him.

"Don't move, Mr. Winters," Agent Levitt ordered.

Cain felt the cold steel pressed against the side of his skull, saw the terror in Caroline's eyes.

"Please, Justin," she begged, "don't make this worse than it needs to be. We have to understand what's going on here."

A tear spilled down her cheek and the sight paralyzed Cain.

Cuffs bound his hands tightly behind his back, and three more agents showed up to assist Levitt with ushering him into the room.

Caroline stood watching, mute with emotion.

Seeing her that way hurt so badly Cain could scarcely think.

Even more painful was the realization that she no longer trusted him.

There was nothing he could do to protect her.

She was lost to him.

Even if he could somehow escape she would not want trust him enough to believe anything he said.

He was just as dead to her as her husband.

Chapter Thirteen

"Mr. Winters, we want you to relax," Agent Levitt said.

Cain didn't look at the man who'd spoken. He had nothing to say to him. His only concern was finding a way to keep Caroline safe whether she ever trusted him again or not.

Anguish charged through him leaving a desolation he had never before experienced. Leaving him with an emptiness that overwhelmed his senses.

"This will keep you calm."

Cain's head snapped up.

Levitt moved toward him with a hypodermic needle in his hand.

"Where did that come from?" another of the agents asked.

"The president wanted to make sure he wouldn't hurt himself," Levitt told him. "A physician is on his way to examine him."

Cain tensed. He couldn't afford to be unconscious or calm. He had to act.

"Whoa!" The two agents on either side of him attempted to pin him to the chair.

The needle pierced his skin. Cain flinched. He felt the sting of whatever toxin the hypodermic contained flowing through his veins.

He relaxed instantly. This would work to his advantage.

His eyes closed and he focused on blocking the effect of the drug. He mentally pictured the chemical receptors in his body, closed each, numbed them to the foreign substance attempting to gain entrance.

He pictured Caroline…safe. He would keep her that way. Nothing would stop him.

Washington, D.C.
Liberty Bar & Grill
Execution

RICHARD O'RILEY sipped his soda water and waited for his guest to arrive at the less than swank Capitol Hill bar. He'd ordered his old friend his preferred drink.

It would end today.

The Collective had sanctioned this final phase of the mission.

O'Riley had only one regret. He hadn't seen this one coming. Maybe he hadn't wanted to. He and Winslow were the last of those who had been there from the beginning. Waylon Galen aside, that is. But that bastard didn't count. If he lived until sundown he would be a lucky man.

But then he'd been lucky for nearly two decades now.

The man was like a cat, appeared to have nine lives.

His luck wouldn't hold out forever. The Collective knew he was still alive now. Finding him wouldn't be that difficult. When he was gone, the Concern would no longer exist. That, to O'Riley's way of thinking, was top priority. The Concern represented the kind of evil America fought hard to uproot so that it would wither and die.

The evil presently coming in O'Riley's direction would not escape that fate either.

O'Riley stood and offered his hand. "Afternoon, Congressman." After the perfunctory handshake, he gestured to the frosty mug of beer. "I took the liberty of ordering for you."

Winslow took a long draw from his glass as soon as he settled at the table. He licked his lips and smiled at his old friend. "It's a scorcher out there today."

"It may rain later," O'Riley repeated what he'd heard on the radio on the way over from his hotel. Might as well trade a bit of small talk.

Winslow made a sound of acknowledgment before gulping another long swallow of his frothy beer.

O'Riley brought his own glass back to his lips wishing like hell the soda water would suddenly morph into bourbon. But he didn't drink anymore. He'd learned his lesson where that habit was concerned. For the first few months after his wife had left him he'd depended far too much on the old reliable companion. He'd almost allowed it to rule him, but he'd recognized the signs and turned his back on all forms of alcohol. It took strict discipline to survive in this business. O'Riley possessed the necessary discipline that so few others did.

That lack of discipline usually cost more than they had anticipated paying.

Too bad no one seemed to realize the price until it was too late.

"So, what's the urgency?" Winslow wanted to know. He removed his finely tailored jacket and laid it across the bench seat on his side of the booth. "I thought we had this operation under control."

"Some compelling new evidence has come to our attention," O'Riley explained. His cellular phone buzzed and he produced a smile for his old comrade. "Excuse me a moment."

He opened the phone and gave his usual gruff bark of a greeting. "O'Riley."

"Sir, Dupree here."

"What've you got for me?" He'd been waiting for this call. In his opinion preparation was the biggest part of the game. No one would ever accuse him of being underprepared.

"Your suspicions were right, sir," Dupree acknowledged. "The page from the Mattson file that Cain provided is a fake."

"Explain." Facts, O'Riley operated on facts more often than hunches. He needed details.

"We tested the paper and it was from a common lot manufactured early this year. No way could it be a part of a file more than ten years old. Someone created the report and placed it in Mattson's stored files."

So, Winslow had set Caroline up. When he couldn't persuade her to go along with his suggestion that she re-allocate Eugenics funding to Genesis, he'd created motivation. He knew how much the woman had loved and respected her father. If the late Congressman Mattson had supported Genesis, so should she. Cain had suspected a setup when he'd read the file. He'd been right.

"Well done. I'll take it from here."

"Yes, sir."

O'Riley snapped his phone closed and dropped it back into his pocket.

Winslow glanced at him. "Everything all right?"

"Right on schedule," O'Riley allowed.

"What's this new evidence you've uncovered?" Winslow prodded, too damned arrogant even to suspect that it involved him. Had he really expected to get away with this?

O'Riley placed both hands on the table in plain sight and looked directly into his old friend's eyes. "We know what you've been up to, Terry. My only question is why?"

Terrence Winslow laughed, the sound short and choked. "What're you talking about, Richard?" he demanded, pretending to be amused. "You know how busy I am. I really don't have time for games. I have a command performance in this afternoon's session." He took another sip of his beer. O'Riley didn't miss the slight tremor in his hand.

"The Collective knows. We all do."

Winslow placed his glass on the table, his gaze heavy

with uncertainty as he met O'Riley's. "Then you shouldn't have to ask the why."

It was O'Riley's turn to laugh. "Tell me it wasn't the money." He leaned forward. "Surely your aspirations were grander than that."

"You know better than to even suggest that money had anything to do with it," Winslow lashed back at him. "Why should a nothing yes-boy like Redmond get to be vice president of the United States? I've done more for this country than he will ever think of doing."

O'Riley shrugged. "That may be, but the bottom line is that you sold us out."

Winslow drew in a deep breath and lifted one shoulder in an answering show of indifference. "We all have a price, *Director O'Riley*. What's yours?"

A new kind of fury boiled up inside O'Riley. He didn't have a price. That's why he'd sacrificed everything. "Tell me where Galen is," he demanded.

"You mean you don't know?" Winslow grinned sheepishly. "Maybe you're losing your touch." He shook his head from side to side, his expression smug. "You think you've got this all figured out. All you have to do is get rid of Caroline now that she's been compromised and the situation will be under control once more." He leaned forward and whispered the rest, "That puts Redmond in charge. Don't you know? Redmond is in it for the power. He'll be easier to manipulate than she was. You can't stop us, Richard. Galen is far too powerful now."

O'Riley squeezed his fingers into fists to keep from

reaching across the table and strangling the bastard. "You set her up with that file. Her father never knew anything about Genesis or Eugenics."

"I'm surprised at you, old friend," Winslow said with utter arrogance. "Usually you're better at this game. Did you really believe I would continue to be happy playing figurehead for the Collective? Galen has far too much more to offer. He'll put me where I belong— in the White House. Be happy I covered for you as long as I did. I could have told him from the beginning what you'd planned with Cain, but I knew it would work to my advantage...keep Caroline Winters off balance emotionally."

He shook his head and sighed. "You really dropped the ball this time. It's so unlike you. Generally you learn the identity of your enemy and you act. But this time you're still going through the motions, trying to ferret out the truth and make your move. You're two steps behind."

"What makes you think I haven't acted already?"

Winslow's expression fell. His eyes abruptly rounded then bulged with fear as realization dawned, or perhaps his insides seized with that truth he spoke of so eloquently.

"What have you done?" he wheezed.

"It's a new designer virus," O'Riley told him, relaxing in his seat. "Lab Three made it just for you. They took your DNA and determined what your weaknesses were. One drop of the virus in your favorite beer was all it took. It works within minutes. It's rushing through your veins now—"

Winslow braced his hands on the table so hard it

shook with the force. He opened his mouth to speak but no words came out.

"Don't bother fighting the effects. It's too late already. The virus has entered your nervous system. Loss of full control over your limbs happened in under ninety seconds. The ability to speak was gone a few seconds later. Soon you'll simply slump forward in your chair and die of asphyxiation as your respiratory system shuts down. An autopsy will reveal nothing conclusive. Simple heart failure. They won't even bother trying to figure out anything beyond that. And this time I'm doing you a favor. Think about it, did you really believe Galen would let you live after he'd used you this way?"

O'Riley tossed a few bills on the table and stood. "Goodbye, old friend."

He walked away without looking back. He had to get word to Cain that the president's status had changed. If it was too late…well, that was a bridge he'd have to cross when he came to it.

By the time he reached his car in the lot outside the restaurant Terrence Winslow was dead.

CAIN ALLOWED his lids to droop so that his guards would think their drug had worked. He slumped forward, careful to keep his respiration slow and even.

"He's out," one of the agents said.

Levitt had left the room. But three remained.

All he had to do was wait for the right moment.

"When is that doctor going to get here?" Agent

Copeland, impatient or nervous, maybe both, paced in front of Cain. "I don't like this."

"The president ordered him confined. We've—"

Cain made his move. He bolted from the chair and knocked Copeland into the agent standing closest to him. The third man made a dive for him, but Cain was too fast. One well-placed blow with his foot and the man hit the floor, unconscious. Swiveling, Cain disabled the other two in the same manner. He quickly retrieved the letter opener from the desk and maneuvered it until he'd picked the lock on the cuffs, freeing his hands.

He used the cuffs to restrain two of the men, locking their hands together around the leg of the armoire. The third he bound with the silk tie he wore.

Confiscating two of the weapons and kicking the last one out of reach, he tucked the two guns into the waistband of his trousers, allowing his jacket to conceal them. He took one agent's cellular phone and communicator so he would be aware of the other agents' movements.

Now all he had to do was find Caroline and keep her safe until…

He didn't know for how long. She was considered the enemy. Keeping her safe might very well equate to staying on the run indefinitely.

It was a chance he was willing to take.

"Madam President."

Caroline looked up to find Agent Levitt hurrying across her office. "Has Dr. Frasier arrived?" she asked. She'd put a call through to Justin's personal physician.

He would come as quickly as he could get away from his clinic, within the hour, he'd promised. Dennis would be arriving later. With late lunch-hour traffic, she hadn't expected Dr. Frasier so quickly. She was glad he was here. She'd done all she could. Having to keep Justin confined…it weighed heavily upon her. She should have talked to him and made sure he understood what was happening.

But she'd been afraid her presence would only antagonize him further. His aggressive reaction had concerned her. She shook off the memories. Why hadn't she realized that all the changes she'd seen in him were pointing to trouble?

"Ma'am, you need to come with me. Mr. Winters has escaped. You're not safe as long as he's on the loose. We've got every agent and all security personnel on the premises watching out for him."

"Escaped?"

Why would he run? Had the confinement pushed him over some edge? She stood, squared her shoulders. "Where is Rupert?" He'd had meetings all day yesterday and all morning today, but he should have returned by now. She needed him in on this.

"He hasn't returned from his visit to the Hill." Levitt gestured to the door. "Please, ma'am, I need to move you to a less easily accessed area until we've contained the threat."

The threat was her husband. Ire twisted inside her but she wasn't foolish enough to ignore the suggestions of her chief of security if he felt compelled to have her move. Her secretary had gone to lunch. Aaron Miller and a number of others on her staff were out as well. Her lunch meeting wasn't for another hour. She relented.

"This way, Madam President." Levitt led the way from the office.

The corridor was oddly quiet, even for lunchtime. Usually there was someone running about, hustling reports or other correspondence between the White House and the Hill.

"Where is everyone?" she asked, frowning. In all the months since she'd taken residence Caroline had not known it to be this deserted.

"I've cleared the area, ma'am."

Caroline stalled, stared at him in bewilderment. "Cleared the area? Why would you do that, Agent Levitt?"

"I'm sorry, ma'am, I'm not authorized to give you that information."

She glared up at him. "Agent Levitt, I'm not going anywhere until you tell me what's going on."

"You…" He swallowed hard. "You don't have clearance for—"

Fury blasted away all other emotion. "I'm the president of the United States," she said tightly. "I have clearance for anything you could possibly know."

Agent Levitt braced his right hand on his weapon. "I don't want to do it this way, ma'am."

As angry as she was at the moment she understood her choices were limited. "You will regret this, Agent Levitt."

He escorted her in the direction of the Situation Room, a kind of war room that monitored the globe 24/7.

"Vice President Redmond is waiting here for you," Levitt added as they neared the secure area.

Redmond? What did he have to do with any of this? Caroline's fury ratcheted up a notch. She should have known.

"Where is Agent Copeland?" she demanded before Levitt opened the door to the Situation Room.

Levitt paused and turned back to her. "I'm afraid he's been injured, ma'am. Mr. Winters took his weapon."

A new kind of shock quaked through her. Surely Justin wasn't involved in this.

"But Justin was restrained," she countered, searching the agent's face for some indication of whether or not she could believe what he'd just told her.

"I'm afraid he isn't who you think he is," Levitt informed her. "The man you brought back from the hospital is not Justin Winters. He's an impostor."

Caroline had thought that nothing else could shock her but she'd been wrong. She shook her head. "That's ridiculous. Now tell me what's going on, Levitt, while you still have the chance. Where is everyone?" The entire West Wing of the White House couldn't have been evacuated without her knowledge.

"Ma'am, you'll have to ask Vice President Redmond about that."

Fury ignited deep in Caroline's belly. How dare Redmond set in motion this kind of backhanded insubordination?

"Ask Mr. Redmond to meet me in the Oval Office," she said pointedly. "I know my way back there."

When she would have turned away Levitt drew his weapon.

Caroline froze.

"Think about what you're doing, Agent Levitt. You don't want to make the same mistake twice."

"They're waiting for you inside, ma'am."

This wasn't supposed to happen here. She was supposed to be safe *here*.

"Drop your weapon."

The harsh command came from behind Levitt. Justin's voice. Relief surged through Caroline making her knees weak. Levitt look as startled as she did relieved.

Levitt relinquished his weapon and adopted the hands-up stance.

"What's going on, Jus—"

A blur of abrupt movement cut off her words. Levitt crumpled to the floor.

"Let's go." Justin snagged her by the arm and started dragging her forward.

"Did you kill him?" Horror echoed through her. She stared up at the man forcing her to run in order to keep up with his pace. *An impostor. Not who you think he is.* The words whirled inside her head.

"I didn't kill him, but he would have killed me."

All the things she'd noticed as different about Justin: his ability to disable a highly trained agent with one swift move, her husband knew nothing of hand-to-hand combat or even self-defense for that matter. Not even a few lessons would have made him this savvy.

Dear God.

She dug in her heels, drawing them both to a halt. When his impatient gaze collided with hers she demanded, "Who are you?"

Chapter Fourteen

"There's no time to explain."

Cain headed straight for the one egress route no one would anticipate. This one led to the parking area outside the West Wing. The passage was originally designed to ensure the presidential driver made it to the car before the president.

Caroline stalled once more. "I'm not going with you."

Cain hesitated at the top of the stairs that spiraled downward, leading to their only hope of escape.

"I can explain." He took her by the shoulders and pulled her closer, allowing her to read his eyes. "Trust me." He mentally echoed the words, urging her to hear. She blinked, startled by the way he could touch her thoughts.

"If we don't go now, we'll both die."

She shook her head. "Just tell me who you are. I have to know…first."

The hurt shimmering in her eyes tore at his chest, fueled the new emotions he had not as of yet conquered.

"My name is Cain. I came to protect you."

She'd thought the truth would somehow provide some sense of relief but she'd been wrong.

She was too stunned to fight the forward momentum as this man—Cain—pulled her along behind him down the winding staircase. The passageway smelled musty with disuse, the lighting was poor.

She blinked. This man—this impostor—had said he'd come to protect her.

But could she believe him? The only thing she knew about him was his name.

No. That wasn't right. She knew him intimately. Knew the feel and taste of his body. Knew the way her own body reacted to his touch…his possession.

He had saved her life…what? Twice now. Maybe he *had* been sent to protect her. But by whom? And why were her own people turning on her in droves?

Where the hell was Rupert? He'd been out of pocket for the better part of the last two days.

None of this made sense.

She stopped, slowing his efforts to hurry once more. "If you only came here to protect me, why the ruse? Why pretend to be my husband?"

He didn't bother to answer her questions. He just kept jogging forward, pulling and tugging her every step of the way.

Why had he made love to her if he was only here to protect her?

Why…?

Belatedly another fact sank through the haze of confusion.

Justin was dead.

This man was not her husband.

He wore the wedding band she'd given her groom on their wedding day.

He pushed through the final doorway, which looked like just another section of wall on the outside. No one would ever have guessed that it opened and led right up to the Oval Office. But it was impossible to open from the outside.

He stopped at the first car they reached and tried the door. When it didn't open he moved to the next.

"How did you get Justin's wedding band?"

Her breath trapped in her lungs. Had he been the one to make those calls? Or maybe he'd forced Justin to make the calls? Justin had to be alive, otherwise how would he know all the things he knew?

"Where's my husband?" she demanded, fury solidifying her courage.

The door on the fourth vehicle he tried opened. He pushed her toward the front seat but she fought to get loose. "I'm not going with you!"

He used his weight to pin her to the car. "Get in the car, now!"

The savage glower emanating from those piercing blue eyes left no doubt that he would use force if she did not obey his order.

She scrambled inside, determined to escape through the passenger door. He was too fast for her. He had the door closed and the locks engaged before she could clamber across the seat.

"You won't get away with this," she warned.

"I already have."

He did something violent to the steering column and seconds later he'd started the engine. He shoved the gear shift into Drive and roared away from the parking slot.

"Get down," he ordered.

"Not until you—"

"Get down now!"

She hunkered down in the seat until he had passed through the gate. He waved and then sped up, leaving the White House grounds behind.

"Where are you taking me?"

Was it possible that this was indeed Justin and that he'd slipped completely over some edge? Had he caused all this confusion—the threats on her life—by following the voices in his head? Did he believe he was someone else?

She thought of the way they'd made love.

This wasn't Justin.

On some level she'd known it all along.

This man was not her husband.

"I'm taking you to safety until I can determine the next step."

The sound of his voice startled her.

She jerked around and stared at the man behind the wheel.

He glanced at her, regret heavy in his expression. "There is no one else you can trust right now. You must believe that if you believe nothing else."

"Where's Justin?" she demanded.

"He's dead. He didn't survive the crash."

Cain sensed he had injured her with that statement but she said nothing. There was no time to discuss the issue further. He drove as fast as he dared knowing that by now word had spread of his escape, as well as her abduction. Those in power would attempt a while longer to keep the events that had transpired out of the media. Time, however, was their enemy.

Just as it was his.

"Where are we going?"

"To the home in Bethesda where you grew up," he said, seeing no reason to keep the truth from her at this point.

She stared at him in disbelief. "Why are we going there?" A new kind of fear stole across her face.

"Your mother is in no danger," he assured quickly. "We're going there because they won't think to look there first."

She said nothing more until they reached her mother's home.

"I don't want her involved if it's going to endanger her in any way."

Apparently she still suspected that he intended to harm her in some way.

"Your mother is in no danger from me and neither are you."

Whether she believed that or not, she got out of the car without force when he'd parked it three houses down from her childhood home. He moved up onto the sidewalk behind her and ushered her toward the safety of the home.

They needed time to develop a strategy. To access necessary funds. To consider who they could trust. Her mother fell into that category. Until they determined who was behind the threat to Caroline…they could trust no one else.

Lora Mattson was not home. Caroline used the hidden spare key and let them into the quiet house.

Cain locked the door behind them and quickly closed the blinds on the front of the house.

He turned to her then. "Sit down and I'll tell you all I know."

As he spoke her face turned paler, her fingers alternately clenched and relaxed, but it was her eyes that did the most damage to his newly discovered emotions. The hurt there cut so deeply he found it hard to draw a breath as he gave her the details of his mission and the threat to her as he knew it.

He did not tell her the facts that would endanger her life, such as his true identity as an Enforcer or about Center.

At the end of his dissertation she sat silently for a moment then said, "I think I need a drink."

Caroline stood on shaky legs and moved toward the sideboard her mother used as a bar. She poured herself a hefty serving of Scotch and took a long sip of it.

She closed her eyes and savored the soothing burn. How was she supposed to believe all that he had told her? It was too…too incredible.

"Do you have proof?" She whirled on him, the alcohol shoring up her courage.

"Look at my face." He gestured to that handsome face that looked exactly like her dead husband's. "Think about the scar. It's gone already. Or hadn't you noticed?"

She blinked and then focused on the place where the scar had been. He was right, it was completely gone now. She *had* noticed. She remembered thinking how strange it was that it seemed to fade. But then she'd dismissed the thought because she'd fallen in love with the man.

He rolled up his sleeve and ripped away the bandage covering the gunshot wound he'd received only a few days ago. The damage was scarcely visible. Impossible. How could he have healed so fast?

After downing another swallow of her drink, she glared at him. "All right, so you're different…genetically superior. But how can you do that?"

"I can do many things, but none of those things changes the fact that I'm helpless to keep you safe for more than a little while longer. We must know who is working against you."

"That's easy." She set her glass aside, figuring anything more than this little buzz would be a bad idea right now. She needed to be able to make decisions…run for her life. "Redmond. He wants me out of the way."

"I think he was just a pawn Winslow was using to get what he wanted."

"Winslow? Congressman Winslow?" What the hell was he talking about? She winced inwardly. Her luncheon engagement would be looking for her. As would Winslow. But, at the moment, she had bigger issues.

"Winslow wanted you to divert funds from Project Eugenics to one called Genesis."

She nodded. "That's right." She'd caught Justin looking at that report. "You read the report. You know what he wanted," she accused.

"Those funds are what this is all about. He used you. Your father's file was a fake."

Disbelief struck her hard. She laughed, a sound sorely lacking in humor. "You expect me to believe that all of this..." She waved her arms magnanimously. "The taunting calls, the letter, the attempts on my life...all of it was because of a possible funding shift?"

He nodded. "I can't tell you anything more about Project Eugenics. Only that its continued existence is essential to this nation's security. No one, not even you in your capacity as the president, would survive the fight to bring it down."

She shook her head. "Wait." She paced the width of the room, trying desperately to grasp his words, but they were far too insane. "You're telling me that my own people would kill me over a few million dollars?"

"A few billion," he corrected. "Part of Eugenics' budget is siphoned from the Pentagon, NSA, NASA. There's much more at stake than you realize."

She strode up to him, hands on hips. "If this project is so damned important then how come I know hardly anything about it? NSA, DOD, no one has ever mentioned it before."

"You weren't ready to know yet," he said bluntly.

"There was no reason to tell you. Everything was under control."

She felt trapped in some kind of time warp where nothing was as it seemed. "Okay, let's say for the sake of conversation that I believe you. Winslow was the bad guy all along. He thought he'd sway my support and get the funding shift. Meanwhile he riles up Redmond in hopes of keeping me distracted. Who was supposed to be behind the calls or those attempts on my life?"

"The same man who likely murdered your husband."

The words sent her stumbling for the closest place to sit. He reached for her, but she refused his help. "How can you say that? The investigation revealed no conclusive evidence of foul play."

The man—Cain—moved closer to her, sat down on the sofa next to her. "Justin Winters met with a known associate of the people who are behind the Genesis Project. He may have been working with them and they felt double-crossed. Whatever the case, the crash was no accident. My people conducted their own investigation before anyone else even knew where the plane had crashed. Your people found only what they were allowed to find."

Her face paled again and she looked at him in sheer horror. "That's how you have Justin's wedding band."

Cain stared at the finger where the gold band resided. It wasn't his…it belonged to her. He pulled it free and offered it to her. "Little else was found."

She snatched the ring from his hand, renewed fury crackling in those wide hazel eyes. "If you know so

damned much then you tell me how to stop Winslow.
How do I even prove any of this?"

"He's probably dead already. My people," he said
carefully, "have likely already taken care of him. It's the
person inside your staff, the person close to you who's
been feeding him the information he has used to get to
you that we need right now."

Confusion lined her smooth brow. "What do you
mean?"

"The calls. It had to be someone close to you to have
your private number…to know just what to do to get to
you. The attempt on your life at that restaurant, who knew
you would be there? Think, Caroline, who is close enough
to know your every move? To change schedules in order
to throw you off, to make you look incompetent?"

Reality settled down on her shoulders like a damp
wool coat. He was right. It had taken someone close to
her to pull off the schedule inconsistencies…to know
her private number.

"Who would know about your father's files? That
you looked to them at times when you remembered
something similar he'd faced in the past?"

A rock of anguish settled heavily in her stomach. Her
secretary had access to her calendar but knew nothing
of Caroline's father's files. It couldn't be. There were
only two people that she trusted on that level besides her
husband and he was dead.

"Rupert and Dennis."

She shook her head in denial even as the names echoed in the room. "I won't believe that one of them would

be involved." She shook her head again. "Dennis was there the day I was shot at. He could have been killed as well.

"Rupert…"

"Was back at the safe house," he finished for her.

Caroline closed her eyes, but she couldn't hide from the truth. Cain—her senses revolted at calling him the name that sounded so alien to her—was right. She scrubbed her hands over her face and through her hair. "God, what do I do?"

Cain remained silent, allowing her to come to her own conclusions. She was thankful for that.

"We don't have much time," she said finally. "But before I can accuse my senior adviser of wrongdoing, of treason, I have to be sure."

Cain nodded. "A test."

Her gaze collided with his. "A test."

IT WAS DARK when headlights flashed across the front of the house. Caroline waited in her father's study. Her mother had been taken to a hotel for safekeeping. She'd told Rupert where the spare key was. He was to meet her there supposedly to discuss the traitor she had discovered and decide on a course of action.

When she heard him fumbling for the key and no other headlights arrived she knew the truth.

Rupert had betrayed her.

She had used the code phrase they had decided on when she first took office. If Caroline ever found herself in a desperate situation of any sort where she needed help immediately she would say the phrase: Mother is expecting you for dinner next Thursday, can you make it?

She and Rupert had laughed at the silliness of it. After all she had the entire Secret Service to protect her, but he had insisted that he know if she ever needed him in a way that she was not free to voice out loud.

Today she had needed him and he'd failed her. He had not called for help…had not taken the measures they had agreed upon if the code phrase was ever initiated. He'd come here alone. To finish the ultimate betrayal.

Agent Copeland and a dozen FBI agents were in the house, around the house, stationed as necessary to protect her. Levitt had told her Copeland was injured but he'd lied. Justin—Cain, she amended—had merely disabled him and restrained him. One call to Copeland's cell phone and she'd won herself an ally. Rather than risk who Levitt had turned among her regular security detail, she had allowed Copeland to call his friends at the Bureau. She sat at her father's desk. A bulletproof vest beneath her blouse protected her torso.

A quiet squeak warned that the front door had opened. Caroline's tension escalated. Agent Copeland and Cain were both in the room with her. Two more agents were in the living room with another hidden in the entry hall. She was safe and yet she was not prepared for this moment.

Part of her still didn't want to believe it could be true. Not Rupert.

Footsteps echoed in the hall, slow, deliberate. But he didn't call out to her. Caroline's heart twisted in anguish.

He suddenly stopped. Her breath caught. A tinkling sound whispered through the darkness.

The rattle of coins. He was jingling his change.

A single teardrop rolled down her cheek. Rupert always did that when he felt at a loss for what to say or do next. Was he having second thoughts now? Did he regret the day he'd agreed to this betrayal?

A succinct snap sounded and then he started forward again, made his way through the dark hall to her father's study and paused at the door. He flipped on the light.

Caroline blinked to adjust to the sudden light.

"Really, Caroline, waiting in the dark? That's a little bizarre, don't you think?"

Dennis.

Confusion scattered the words she had prepared to hurl at Rupert. "Dennis, what're you doing here?"

He waved the gun in his hand, the barrel leveling on her in the end. "I showed up at your office as I promised and Rupert was rushing out the door insisting that you were in trouble." Dennis shrugged. "When he told me what had happened and that he had to call in backup, I knew I had to take care of this myself."

Her head moved from side to side of its own volition. "Where's Rupert?" This couldn't be. Dennis was her friend. She'd known him forever…told him everything.

He cocked his head toward the door. "He's in the car. But I don't think he's in the mood to talk, he's pretty much dead."

Hurt swelled in her chest and she stood before she

had the good sense to stay still. They'd told her not to move from her position.

"What're you doing, Dennis? How could you betray me?"

He glanced around the room. "Before we get into that, where's your lover? I know he left with you. You know, I knew that guy wasn't Justin the moment you told me you'd found him."

"He's dead."

"Yeah, Justin's dead all right." Dennis nodded, his expression mocking. "But where's the stand-in, the one who got you off when old Justin couldn't?"

Caroline shuddered with too many emotions to separate. "You bastard. He's dead too. Didn't Levitt tell you? He killed him." Caroline knew that Levitt was in custody in the private conference room. Redmond was there as well, although he was not in official custody. Her most trusted member of the Cabinet, Secretary of State Hall, was interrogating the two in order to determine what he could about their respective parts in this matter. The latest technology in lie detection had been brought over by the CIA. No one else at the White House was aware of anything that had happened this day. The injured agents had been sent to Walter Reed for twenty-four-hour monitoring under guard.

No one would know of any of this…until Caroline was ready for them to know…if ever.

"Actually, now that you mention it, I didn't see Levitt." He glanced around the room once more. "He's not hanging around here anywhere pretending to be your friend now, is he? He'd better not. How do you think I screwed with your calendar all those times?"

"There's no one here but us," Caroline said, fury boiling beneath her words. "I'm on the run, or didn't you know it? Redmond is meeting with the Cabinet right now to try and invoke the Twenty-Fifth."

Dennis nodded. "Oh yeah. I do recall that Levitt had the impression the good old VP wanted you out of the way."

"Tell me why," she urged, not only for the ears listening but also for her own peace of mind. She had to know why her closest friend had betrayed her.

"Gosh, Caroline, I wish I could give you some higher moral reasoning but you see, it's nothing like that. It's simply about the money. Waylon Galen made me an offer I couldn't refuse. All I had to do was make life miserable for you while his busy little soldiers—like Winslow—did his dirty work." Dennis placed his free hand over his heart in emphasis of his words. "It was so easy. Between what you told me and what Justin babbled on about, I had all the ammunition I needed."

"Justin? When did Justin talk to you about me?"

"When we first became lovers," Dennis said pointedly. "Don't you know anything?"

The weight of that statement forced her back down into her chair.

"Don't feel bad, it didn't last long. Apparently Justin didn't like men any more than he did women. I even tried to recruit him to help me get you out of the way. Galen made him a great offer as well, but he refused.

Had some stupid loyalty to you even if he couldn't bring himself to have sex with you."

Caroline held up her hands. "I don't want to hear any more." She couldn't bear it. It was too much.

"Oh, come on, babe. Don't you want to know just how involved the process of removing a president from office can be? You only have a couple of choices, make 'em look crazy or assassinate 'em. Hell, you beat us at every turn. Between you and that special bodyguard they—whoever the hell *they* is—sent you, we couldn't win for losing."

He shrugged again. "I guess I'm just gonna have to do this the old-fashioned way." He laughed as he pulled the slide back on the weapon in his hand. "I've never had to kill anyone before tonight. Hell, I even forgot to put the clip back in the damned thing after accidentally ejecting it. Had to stop in the hallway and do that. But you see, Winslow didn't follow through so I have no choice." He looked at the gun then at her. "Recognize it? It was your father's. They're going to find you and the note you're about to write, of course. It'll be perfect. I'll tell them all about how I tried to console you but you were determined to end your life when you lost your husband for the second time. And we do have all these other mix-ups to toss in."

"Don't come any closer," she warned. As much as she hated Dennis right now, she didn't want him to die. The idea that he'd hurt Rupert made her want to scream with agony and at the same time she wanted to shake some sense into this man who'd always been so levelheaded. How could she have missed this side of him? He'd always seemed so far above greed…above this kind of evil. How could she not have seen him for what he was? "Put the gun down, Dennis."

He laughed, that ugly, hateful sound that spoke of pure evil. "Make it easy on yourself, doll, you're already dead. You just gotta write the note."

"Dennis, please—"

He took another step and a gunshot exploded in the room. Dennis staggered back a step, shock registering on his face. He stared down at the leaking bullet hole in the center of his chest and then he crumpled to the floor, the weapon he'd wielded sliding across the floor.

Caroline stumbled back from the desk. She struggled to breathe. Oh God. The car. He'd said Rupert was in the car…*pretty much dead.* "Rupert!"

FBI agents descended upon the room. Cain climbed from beneath the desk where he'd taken up a position, ultimately shooting Dennis through the wood panel that had shielded him from view. He would later explain that his heightened senses had alerted him to precisely when to fire.

Caroline found Rupert still alive…barely. Someone called an ambulance. She held her beloved friend and begged him not to die on her.

There were so many people in her mother's yard. A man speaking to Cain. Blue lights flickering. The sound of a siren wailing in the distance.

Paramedics were suddenly at the car, moving Rupert. Her hands went to her mouth to hold back the cries that welled in her throat. Only then did she notice the blood. So much blood.

She scrambled out of the car to follow the paramedics. From across the lawn her gaze locked with Cain's. For two beats she couldn't move…she could only feel the flood of emotions emanating from him.

The ambulance was leaving…she had to go.

Caroline, along with Copeland and another of her security detail, boarded a second ambulance without looking back. She had no way of knowing that she would never see the face of Justin Winters again.

Chapter Fifteen

Oval Office
One month later...

"Madam President, you won't regret giving us your full support." Governor Kyle Remmington, a Republican currently representing the great state of Colorado and the newly elected head of the Collective, offered his hand.

"I'm confident I won't." Caroline shook his hand firmly and then reached for the other man's. "Director O'Riley, it was a pleasure to meet you. I hope you know that I'll be visiting your facility in the near future. I'd like to see those funds at work."

Remmington and O'Riley exchanged a look, then O'Riley smiled. "Come anytime, President Winters. I think you'll be impressed."

"I already am."

Caroline walked the men to the door and exchanged the final pleasantries. O'Riley paused before leaving. "Give me a moment," he said to the governor. Remmington nodded his understanding. O'Riley turned back to Caroline when his companion had moved out of hearing range. "Tell me, Madam President," he said with emphatic formality, "what can I do for you? I want to show my gratitude in a tangible manner for your support."

She smiled, barely holding back the tremble that quaked her lips. "I appreciate the thought, Director O'Riley. But I'm afraid there's nothing you can do for me." She wasn't clear what he was asking, but she didn't want him to feel indebted. She'd made this decision based on the good of the nation; what he could or could not offer her played no role in the matter.

O'Riley winked. "You'd be surprised what I can do," he said enigmatically.

He walked away with that mysterious statement hanging in the air. Caroline moved back to her desk and reviewed the afternoon's calendar. She sighed. She so missed Rupert. But he wouldn't be back to work for another two weeks. Those last days before he'd been shot, she had learned he'd been distracted by his own investigation into the strange happenings around Caroline. He would be on leave longer if her mother had anything to do with it. The two were now officially dating. Caroline thanked God he was alive.

Memories of that night descended upon her before she could stop them as she usually did. She thought of how Dennis and Agent Levitt had betrayed her. How Redmond himself had almost fallen into the trap. Samuel Hall's interrogation had proven that Redmond hadn't been personally involved. He'd been arrogant and uncooperative, but that was as far as his participation had gone.

Winslow had been the middleman between the White House and the Concern. Dr. Waylon Galen had hoped to regain the power he'd lost so many years ago. His bitterness had turned him evil. His vicious machinations had cost numerous lives. Though he had not been found, his plans had been thwarted. He was impotent without the funding he had sought. They'd also learned that the Concern was responsible in great part for the increasing antagonism in Colombia against the United States. The facility Galen had built there had been located and dismantled.

The knowledge that Justin had not betrayed her in the end relieved Caroline. Dennis had preyed upon his uncertainty about his sexuality. He had used him and then allowed him to be murdered by Galen's people when he would have given Caroline the evidence to stop these atrocities months ago.

And then there was Cain. The man she hadn't even really known, but with whom she'd fallen deeply, deeply in love. Or maybe it was simply lust. He'd brought her back to life, had touched her as no other man had. She'd told herself that she truly believed him to be her husband and that's why she'd made love with him, when the truth was she'd suspected something all along, but she'd wanted him so badly she had ignored her instincts.

Now he was gone.

She'd wanted to ask O'Riley to tell her what had become of Cain since he had disobeyed the direct order to eliminate her. O'Riley didn't like that his man had shared that truth with her, but he'd explained that he'd done what he had to do to protect Center. In a twisted sort of way she recognized his admission as a sign of extreme loyalty. But the more human side of her wanted to slap him for having the nerve to play God.

But she wouldn't ask. Couldn't ask. It hurt too much even to allow enough hope to speak his name out loud.

Caroline pushed away the thoughts and focused on the future. As far as the world knew, her husband had died of an undetected brain aneurysm that night in her mother's home—a delayed result of the plane crash. Her brief reunion with him had been a mere godsend as far as the world knew.

Soon they would learn that he'd returned to her just long enough to leave her with a gift to remember him by.

She was pregnant.

Something else she had chosen not to share with O'Riley. Of course, he would know soon enough. But she wasn't worried. He had what he wanted now. She had guaranteed Center's funding throughout her term. If he so much as attempted to touch a hair on her child's head, she would reverse that decision.

"Madam President."

Caroline cleared her throat and met her secretary's expectant gaze. "Yes, Barbara."

"You have a visitor. He says that he's an old acquaintance of yours."

Bewildered, Caroline shook her head. "What's his name, Barbara?" That would help. What was with her secretary this afternoon? Or maybe it was Caroline. She was still a little off her game.

"He said his name is Cain."

Anticipation roared like a lion through Caroline. "Cain?"

"He didn't give a last name. Agent Copeland cleared him through security."

Copeland was the only one of her staff who knew about Cain.

"Send him in." The whispered words were scarcely more than a shadow of thought. Somehow Barbara understood and rushed away to do her president's bidding.

When the door opened again a man she didn't recognize entered the office.

Caroline's hand went to her throat as her breath trapped there. He was tall, broad-shouldered, muscular. Blondish brown hair. But she didn't recognize the face. The eyes…the eyes she knew. Piercing blue…sky-blue. Cain's eyes.

She had moved around her desk before she even realized she'd stood. "It's you," she murmured, afraid to believe, but knowing in her heart it was him.

He nodded. "It's me."

She recognized that voice. It was the one he'd spoken in that last night…his true voice.

Before good sense could kick in she'd reached up and touched his handsome face. "This is the real you?"

He nodded.

She traced the lean chiseled cheeks and the strong brow and chin, the slender blade of a nose. Lastly her fingers trailed over firm, full lips. The same lips that had kissed her and brought her such pleasure.

He kissed her fingers. "I've missed you, Caroline."

She gasped, drew her fingers away. "But you left and I thought…"

"O'Riley gave me a special dispensation," he explained as he took her hands in his. "I'm kind of in reserve status now. I'll live a normal life wherever I choose, but if Center ever needs me I'll make myself available. It's a rare liberty."

Hope bloomed in her chest. "And where do you choose to live this new, normal life?" Her heart pounded so hard she feared it would jump out of her chest any moment.

"I choose to live it with you." He tugged her closer. "If you want me."

If she wanted him! Caroline draped her arms around his neck and smiled up at him, her lips trembling with relief…with happiness. "I think you know the answer to that."

One corner of that sexy mouth tilted into an answering grin. He leaned down and whispered against her ear, his warm breath making her shiver. "I know the proceedings in this room are recorded for posterity, otherwise I'd make love to you right now on that big, gleaming desk."

She stood on tiptoe and whispered back, "For your information, there's one narrow spot against the wall on the other side of the room that the monitor doesn't catch." Her body was already heating up at the idea of having him sink deeply inside her. "Apparently a previous president discovered the blind spot. Made headlines with it if I remember correctly."

"Show me." Cain nipped her earlobe.

She tugged him toward that blind spot on the far side of the room. "There's something I have to tell you first," she murmured secretively.

"What's that?" He pressed her against the wall.

"Closer," she whispered. "You might not be out of the monitor's range yet." Though she knew he was.

He flattened against her, his hard body making her gasp with anticipation. "Close enough?"

She nodded as another wave of sweet ecstasy washed over her and they weren't even skin to skin yet.

"What was it you had to tell me?" He kissed her neck, raked his lips over her skin.

She shivered. "Maybe I'll tell you afterward."

"That'll work." His mouth claimed hers and there was no more talk. But talk wasn't necessary. Cain already knew...Caroline was having his child.

THE LIMOUSINE sped across the beltway, carrying O'Riley and the new head of the Collective toward the airport. O'Riley couldn't help feeling a little proud of himself. He'd gotten what he wanted. And he was damned sure she'd gotten exactly what she wanted.

"You think allowing Cain to go on reserve status was a good idea?" Remmington asked.

"Absolutely."

"What about the child?"

"Well," O'Riley offered, watching the landscape as it whizzed by. "I don't see how we can begrudge the president the child of her late husband."

Remmington frowned then enlightenment dawned. "Ah, I see your point. If the child went missing she would cry foul and the whole world might learn about…us."

"Exactly."

Remmington nodded. "Very good, O'Riley. She'll keep us happy to protect her child."

"In a manner of speaking." He grinned. "And it never hurts to have an inside man in the White House. Especially one in the right bed."

Remmington seemed satisfied with that explanation.

The truth was Caroline Winters deserved the man she loved and the child they had created together. If O'Riley had learned nothing else in this life, it was that nothing should stand in the way of true love.

Hell, maybe he was just getting soft.

"What about Galen?" Remmington asked. "Can we consider him out of the game?"

O'Riley shrugged. "He's alive. As long as he's alive he poses some threat, but he's rather impotent with no funding and no power. To my knowledge he doesn't have a fan still breathing in this country or in any other. If he manages to survive it will only be by the grace of some former world power who can't offer him much more than asylum."

"So the storm has passed?"

"The storm has passed. Galen can't touch us. He doesn't have a single link left to Center. There's no way he can get to us now."

"Good."

The words reverberated in O'Riley's head. Even as he'd uttered them he'd known it was—in part—a lie. There was one link…however obscure. No one even remembered her. Galen wouldn't think of her either. Even if he did he would only recall that she had been eliminated as a failure. That she had actually been mainstreamed was a secret O'Riley would take to his grave. Even way back then he hadn't had the heart to kill a kid.

Maybe he'd always been soft on some level.

Besides she remembered nothing of Center. She posed no threat. She had been a failure. Even if by some stretch of the imagination Galen found her…it would prove nothing. She was of no value and certainly represented no threat.

O'Riley shook off that whole line of thinking. No way Galen could even suspect. That one missing link was safe. Even O'Riley didn't know where she was.

No one knew.

* * * * *

Look for MAN OF HER DREAMS,
the chilling finale of THE ENFORCERS *trilogy*
coming next month from Harlequin Intrigue!

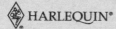 HARLEQUIN®

INTRIGUE®

**Has a brand-new trilogy
to keep you
on the edge of your seat!**

Better than all the rest...

THE ENFORCERS

BY

DEBRA WEBB

JOHN DOE ON HER DOORSTEP
April

EXECUTIVE BODYGUARD
May

MAN OF HER DREAMS
June

Available wherever Harlequin Books are sold.

www.eHarlequin.com

HIMOHD

Signature Select™

SPOTLIGHT

National bestselling author

JOANNA WAYNE

The Gentlemen's Club

A homicide in the French Quarter of New Orleans has attorney Rachel Powers obsessed with finding the killer. As she investigates, she is shocked to discover that some of the Big Easy's most respected gentlemen will go to any lengths to satisfy their darkest sexual desires. Even murder.

A gripping new novel… coming in June.

Bonus Features, including:

Author Interview, Romance— New Orleans Style, and Bonus Read!

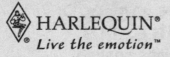

HARLEQUIN®

® *Live the emotion*™

www.eHarlequin.com   SPTGCR

eHARLEQUIN.com

The Ultimate Destination for Women's Fiction

For **FREE online reading,** visit
www.eHarlequin.com now and enjoy:

Online Reads
Read **Daily** and **Weekly** chapters from
our Internet-exclusive stories by your
favorite authors.

Interactive Novels
Cast your vote to help decide how these
stories unfold...then stay tuned!

Quick Reads
For shorter romantic reads, try our
collection of Poems, Toasts, & More!

Online Read Library
Miss one of our online reads?
Come here to catch up!

Reading Groups
Discuss, share and rave with other
community members!

For great reading online,
visit www.eHarlequin.com today!

INTONL04R

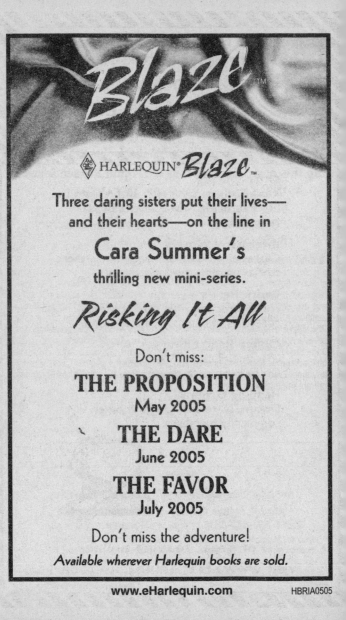

Blaze™

HARLEQUIN® Blaze™

Three daring sisters put their lives—
and their hearts—on the line in

Cara Summer's

thrilling new mini-series.

Risking It All

Don't miss:

THE PROPOSITION
May 2005

THE DARE
June 2005

THE FAVOR
July 2005

Don't miss the adventure!

Available wherever Harlequin books are sold.

www.eHarlequin.com   HBRIA0505

If you enjoyed what you just read,
then we've got an offer you can't resist!

Take 2 bestselling love stories FREE!

Plus get a FREE surprise gift!

Clip this page and mail it to Harlequin Reader Service®

IN U.S.A.	IN CANADA
3010 Walden Ave.	P.O. Box 609
P.O. Box 1867	Fort Erie, Ontario
Buffalo, N.Y. 14240-1867	L2A 5X3

YES! Please send me 2 free Harlequin Intrigue® novels and my free surprise gift. After receiving them, if I don't wish to receive anymore, I can return the shipping statement marked cancel. If I don't cancel, I will receive 4 brand-new novels each month, before they're available in stores! In the U.S.A., bill me at the bargain price of $4.24 plus 25¢ shipping and handling per book and applicable sales tax, if any*. In Canada, bill me at the bargain price of $4.99 plus 25¢ shipping and handling per book and applicable taxes**. That's the complete price and a savings of at least 10% off the cover prices—what a great deal! I understand that accepting the 2 free books and gift places me under no obligation ever to buy any books. I can always return a shipment and cancel at any time. Even if I never buy another book from Harlequin, the 2 free books and gift are mine to keep forever.

181 HDN DZ7N
381 HDN DZ7P

Name		(PLEASE PRINT)	
Address		Apt.#	
City		State/Prov.	Zip/Postal Code

Not valid to current Harlequin Intrigue® subscribers.

Want to try two free books from another series?
Call 1-800-873-8635 or visit www.morefreebooks.com.

* Terms and prices subject to change without notice. Sales tax applicable in N.Y.
** Canadian residents will be charged applicable provincial taxes and GST
   All orders subject to approval. Offer limited to one per household.
   ® are registered trademarks owned and used by the trademark owner and or its licensee.

INT04R   ©2004 Harlequin Enterprises Limited

HARLEQUIN

INTRIGUE

Like a phantom in the night comes

ECLIPSE

GOTHIC ROMANCE

Each month we offer you
a classic blend of chilling suspense
and electrifying danger.

June 2005
MYSTIQUE
CHARLOTTE DOUGLAS

July 2005
GHOST HORSE
PATRICIA ROSEMOOR

August 2005
URBAN SENSATION
DEBRA WEBB

Don't miss a single spine-tingling tale!

Available wherever Harlequin books are sold.

www.eHarlequin.com   HIME

SPOTLIGHT

**A NEW 12-book series featuring
the reader-favorite Fortune family
launches in June 2005!**

THE
**F RTUNES
OF TEXAS:**
Reunion

Cowboy at Midnight

by *USA TODAY* bestselling author

ANN MAJOR

Rancher Steven Fortune considered
himself lucky. He had a successful
ranch, good looks and many female
companions. But when the contented
bachelor meets events planner
Amy Burke-Sinclair, he finds
himself bitten by the love bug!

**The Fortunes of Texas:
Reunion—**
The power of family.

**Exclusive Extras!
Family Tree...
Character Profiles...
Sneak Peek**

Silhouette®
Where love comes alive™

Visit Silhouette Books at www.eHarlequin.com   FTRCM

Return to

McCALLS' MONTANA

this spring
with

B.J. DANIELS

Their land stretched for miles across
the Big Sky state…all of it hard-earned—
none of it negotiable. Could family ties
withstand the weight of lasting legacy?

AMBUSHED!
May

HIGH-CALIBER COWBOY
June

SHOTGUN SURRENDER
July

Available wherever Harlequin Books are sold.

www.eHarlequin.com   HIA